# Storyteller Journal of

Started in 2017

Volume 7 · Issue 12 · December 2023

ISBN: 978-1-955783-13-2

MW01503810

**EDITOR**
Shay Shivecharan

**COPY EDITOR**
Michael Birk

**ASSOCIATE EDITORS**
Gabriel McLeod, Joshua Mahn

**COVER PHOTOGRAPHY**
Jeannie Albers

**FEATURED ON COVER**
Alan Sincic, Nicholas Michael Reeves

 threeowlspublishing.com/storytellerjournal

 storyteller@threeowlspublishing.com

 fb.com/storytellerjournal

 @storytellerjournal

---

Storyteller is a publication of **Three Owls Publishing**

THREE OWLS
PUBLISHING

# JEANNIE ALBERS

*Art Director & Photographer*

JEANNIEALBERS.COM

# POETRY

# FICTION

# NONFICTION

# CONTRIBUTORS

## Alan Sincic

A teacher at Valencia College, short stories of mine have appeared in *New Ohio Review*, *The Greensboro Review*, *Boulevard Online*, *The Saturday Evening Post*, *Grist*, *Big Fiction*, *Terrain.org*, and elsewhere. In recent years my fiction and nonfiction have won contests sponsored by *Hunger Mountain*, *Meridian*, *Orison*, *The Texas Observer*, *Driftwood Press*, *The Plentitudes*, *Prism Review*, *Pulp Literature*, *Broad River Review* and others.

 www.alansincic.com

## Darryl Pickett

Darryl Pickett is a former Walt Disney Imagineer and theme park consultant. He left Winter Garden in 2020 to rejoin family in Albuquerque, New Mexico. He wrote *The Angel and Elvis* in honor of his friendship with the late Suzanna Leigh whom he met 13 years ago.

 @flippyshark

## Vanessa Frances

Vanessa Frances is the author of three poetry collections, written through her teenage and young adult life. She holds a BA in Digital Journalism and Media from Pennsylvania State University and is pursuing an MS in Environmental Law from Vermont Law and Graduate School. She works as a marketer, managing editor, musician, and dog walker. .

 @fad* @fad* @faaemusic

## Joe Tankersley

Joe Tankersley is a storyteller, futurist, and former Walt Disney Imagineer. His short stories have appeared in New Maps, Disruption Magazine, Solutions, Conscious Company Magazine, and the anthology *Aftershocks and Opportunities* edited by Rohit Talwar. *Reimagining Our Tomorrows, Making Sure Your Future Doesn't Suck*, Joe's collection of speculative futures vignettes, was published in 2018. Joe lives in Winter Springs, Florida, where he waits patiently for rising sea levels to transform his suburban backyard into beachfront property.

 www.joetankersley.com

# CONTRIBUTORS

## Nicholas Michael Reeves

Raconteur. Crossword maven. Writer of *Letters to the Dead*. An aspirant Warhol of the poem. I love the taste of words. Taste, for instance, *a fogged window, an abandoned railroad, a lone crow, coffee-stained postcards*. Then ask the question: Where would civilization be if we didn't write about them? Then take a deep breath. I'm no hero or anything. Someone has to translate the birdsong, interpret the silence, and eavesdrop on you—stranger.

 @nicholasmichaelreeves

## Aaron Morrison

Aaron was born during the great __natural disaster__ in the _season_ of _year_. He spends his free time exploring _unusual location__ and raising domesticated __fictional creature(plural)__. One day, he would like to _verb_ his way to _place_ and try the various _noun(plural)__.

 @theaaronmorrison

🌐 linktr.ee/TheAaronMorrison

## Gabriel McLeod

Gabriel is an artist and writer that hails from the Deep South and currently resides in a moment of time at a corner of Earth known as Florida. He found meaning through the escape in creativity at an early age and has been chasing that feeling ever since. He is honored to be part of the *Storyteller* family.

 @gabrielmcleod

## Joshua Mahn

Joshua Mahn is being pursued by a fearsome beast just outside of your house, immediately after you fall asleep. Please leave some refreshments on the patio suitable for both him and the beast, if you should think of it

 @joshmahnwrites

# CONTRIBUTORS

### Clay Waters

Clay Waters lived in Florida until the age of four and returned to find it hadn't changed a bit. Three of his six memories from that first stop involve the alphabet, which in retrospect was a bit of a tell. He has had stories and poetry published in The Santa Barbara Review, The Headlight Review, Green Hills Literary Lantern, and Poet Lore, as well as Storyteller.

@clayman45123

Storyteller is always looking for new voices and fresh perspectives. Submissions can be made to: storytellersubmissions@gmail.com

# BOB SANDERS

## by Alan Sincic

### The lightning struck. The rain

The purpose of this story is to make you want to be friends with the author. Is it good enough yet? Has he succeeded? His name is Bob Sanders and he lives at 2624 Wicker Lane, New Haven, CT 04720 and he would love it if you would come by afterwards for a drink or, if you are not the drinking kind, a cup of hot tea or some cocoa.

### The rain fell to the ground. "Heavens to Betsy," said Betsy

So just kick back and relax. Bob cannot begin to tell you how excited he is that you chose him over all those other great writers like Shakespeare and Hemmingway you could be reading right now instead of him. What a classy person you are turning out to be! Bob will do his darndest to live up to your high expectations for him and, in the larger sense, for literature as a whole.

### said Betsy with a shake of her blonde head,

It goes without saying that Bob here will be as light or as heavy as you like because by golly you are the customer and the customer is always right.

### a shake of her head that was blonde,

So if you would like a different noun or verb or whatever then just ask. Bob's been slaving all day over these nouns and verbs his aim being to please but hey – plenty more where that came from! No problem. If there's a word that has been misspelled, then let's work together to catch it now, early on, before things get even more out of control. Is there an indentation where there should not be an indentation? Then Bob will have that indentation removed, by force if necessary, and at whatever cost to his own personal vision.

### Betsy with her blonde hair shaking on her head that was a normal color

And at no extra cost to yourself. Wow. And without having to rustle up a single word on your own. Lucky for you! But you deserve it! Bob is more than happy to give you a well-earned rest while he struggles to provide you with the snappy details and the gruff-but-lovable characters that you have come to expect of him, the quirky down home imagery that is beaten out of him for the sole delight and amusement of ... oops. Bob seems to have more nouns and verbs than he realized. Gracious. Bob has been very tired lately. But Bob is not a complainer.

### said bald Betsy

Because nobody wants to be friends with a complainer. Friendship is built on trust. And you can trust Bob when he tells you it's not as glamorous as you think this life of the raconteur. Henry James suffered from bad digestion. Ernest Hemmingway broke three ribs in a plane crash on the African veldt. Bob Sanders can no longer recite his poetry within a hundred feet of the lobby of the Bedford Cineplex or affiliated entities in the State of Connecticut but is Bob Sanders going to let that throw a monkey wrench into the burning fire of his (Bob Sander's) heart? In your dreams!

**Betsy as she ran through the rain.** "Wait up, you handsome-looking Detective Sands who only recently became my boyfriend," she said. Suddenly

So fasten your seatbelts because here we go.

**"Bang –**

If you are a pregnant woman, a person with a heart condition, or a child under 42", you just might want to step out of line right now before we kick this baby up into overdrive

**"Bang-Bang!" Betsy screamed. Detective Sands went crashing through a window**

If you are reading this and happen to be a movie producer that thing about the window breaking don't be worried. You could get a stunt window and a stunt person so that nobody would get hurt. And an action star like Burt Reynolds would be good in the part of the Detective because he does all his own stunts. That way you save money.

**as glass went flying everywhere. "Ouch," said hard-boiled Detective Sands**

Sometimes they fly the writer to Hollywood to be there on the set while they make the movie. A good idea, since the writer knows how the words go and could even explain to Burt Reynolds what he (the writer) was thinking during the writing of the story.

**he said to his humorous sidekick Spongy. "I have just
been shot by a bullet and gone crashing through a
window."**

Some writers, like Shakespeare or like, say, Bob Sanders for example,
have done a little acting in their own spare time and in, like, an
emergency, if, say, Burt Reynolds broke his leg or something, they could
step right in and do the part themselves. Plus they already know what
happened in the story. A double savings!

**"Goodness gracious," said Spongy humorously,**

So you're wondering would Bob object to the using of for instance his
likeness on the billboards for the movie the answer would be no if it was
done out of friendship and not Hollywood type friendship either but real
friendship. For a friend Bob would be more than happy to visit the TV
talk shows and such to share humorous anecdotes about the movie, the
book, the writing process, hopes and dreams and wishes and so forth.
And as far as a limo for the Oscars and all go, not to worry. Good old
Bob Sanders would just as soon drive his own self in his own beat-up old
down-home car and if you ask why, because that's the kind of guy he is
is why.

**"*Ouch* is right, you hard-boiled, brown-haired, six-foot
two-inch detective, you," said Spongy jokingly**

Though that not happening till the movie was done,

**to the Cleveland-born Detective Sands,**

which depending on the book being done

**an '87 graduate of Sandusky Community College**

being depending on the individual sentences

**with a degree in Animal Husbandry**

like this one

**and a minor in**

making it to the end without running out of the stuff that goes into them in the first place, meaning

**Detectiving.**

words. Mercy. Talk about a pressure. But a good pressure in Bob's case a fun pressure Bob being a fun-loving free-wheeling kind of guy. Creativity is Bob's middle name. Carpe Deum! Just think of the words in all the other stories that Bob has already produced, like that one about the man drinking the cup of coffee and trying to get it to just the right amount of cream on the inside. You liked that story, didn't you? Go back and look at that story. Compare the two stories. Do you think that there has been a falling off in Bob's talent? Maybe he was never very good to begin with. Maybe he should go back to the job in the hardware store. Is this what it would take to make you happy?

**Bang! The owner of the hardware store clutched his breast and crumpled to the**

Oy vey! Sakes alive. Cowabunga. It would be very easy for Bob to say "Go on, charge on, charge on ahead and gallop right over the feelings of Bob Sanders. You are a daring and artistic soul. Please do not bruise the tip of your finger as you reach for another toasted cheese puff." It would be easy to say that but Bob not is going to say that because Bob is a peach of a guy.

**ground. Down to the ground he crumpled as Detective Sands**

A peach of a guy just warning you not to be fooled by friends who pretend to be friends but bail when you need them the most.

**good old Detective Sands along with Spongy and his (Detective Sand's, not Spongy's) girlfriend Betsy jumped into their fancy racecar to racecar themselves away from the broken glass in the other sentence and onto the hardware store, just in time to catch the pretty checkout girl**

So be careful. You've gotten (those of you who are innocent) a warm feeling these last few paragraphs we've been together. But life is more than a warm feeling. A bunch of words on a page is no substitute for love. And what good is a warm feeling if you've got nobody to get warm and feely about? So snap out of it.

**standing over the body with a smoking gun in her hand. "Come with me," commanded Detective Sands**

You don't want to grow old and die all alone, now do you? Goodness gracious. There's a great big old world out there just full of people wanting to be your friend. So get cracking!

**"Me. Come with me," commanded Detective Sands commandingly. "Like on a date?" said the attractive slim-figured hardware checkout girl to**

"But I don't know how to make friends," you say. "I am so pathetic." Don't be silly. If you were to start, say, with somebody you already know (like say Bob Sanders), then you could just write them a letter say how much you are liking whatever it is you happen to be doing this moment an example being, say, reading this story by

**the ruggedly handsome detective**

Bob Sanders.

In the letter you could say how anybody who managed to come up with such attractive nouns and verbs and stuff must also probably be an attractive person in the physical sense, direct and in person. In the letter you could say how refreshing it is to come across a writer who is so open and personable. Remember, on the printed page, Bob may not seem to be such a vividly realized character, but in person you would find him much more concrete and specific than anybody could have expected. Even more so.

> "Yes, yes – a date," said the ruggedly handsome detective as he swept her up into his rugged arms and gave her a big kiss. "Wow!" said girlfriend number one to girlfriend number two, "another extra girlfriend for my boyfriend Detective Sands!"

Gosh. And if you were a letter and your car was an envelope, you could just up and mail yourself to 2624 Wicker Lane exit 27 off I-75 south! Wouldn't that be something?

> Up into his other arm she jumped, the one not holding the pretty checkout girl. "You are just too much man for one woman!"

If you get here and Bob doesn't answer, come right on in anyway and make yourself at home. The key is under the garden gnome with the wheelbarrow, over to the left of the mailbox. There's a carafe of pasteurized orange juice in the fridge, cups in the cabinet above the sink. Help yourself to any snacks (the tropical fruit and nut mix is particularly good) and feel free to peruse Bob's collection of 1930's roadside diner placemats.

> "Three cheers for Detective Sands," cheers the crowd. The Pope looks down from his balcony and waves. Even though he is wounded, Detective Sands

If you are a publisher (or would like to be one), feel free to check the second drawer from the bottom of Bob's dresser where you can find his unpublished poems, notes, hopes, wishes and dreams. Help yourself! What a surprise it will be when Bob finds his work suddenly appearing in print! And in your magazine!

**still manages, though wounded, seriously wounded, to throw chocolates to the busload of orphans pulling up to the crime scene. "Look at that arm," exclaims Hall of Fame Orioles third baseman**

Bob's dog Scooter will be delighted to lick your hand and scamper gaily round your pant cuffs because any friend of Bob's is a friend of Scooters. If you are the appropriate gender (entirely your decision Bob not being one to pressure) feel free to slip into something comfortable, pour yourself a glass of wine, and drape yourself seductively across the Barco-lounger to wait for Bob to

**ejaculates Hall of Fame Orioles third baseman Cal Ripkin, Jr. admiringly: "Hell of an arm!" "Good work, Sandy-man," barks gruff Police Commander Sean Connery co-starring Harrison Ford as Spongy. Suddenly**

to pop up, for Bob to pop up. Or slip into the kitchen bake him a hot apple pie an apron slung over your shoulder to wipe the crumbs from his cheek when

**the wounded Detective Sands crumples to the ground.**

**How brave of him to make it even this far. The
girlfriends scoop him up into their four breasts and
carry him up the steps to**

wipe the crumbs, wipe the crumbs from his cheek when he finally
arrives. If you're unpacking your suitcase in the front bedroom you
might want to lay out your socks and underwear on the bed first

**the podium where General Douglas MacArthur
presents the Congressional Medal of**

so that you'll be more comfortable. If you're giving birth don't hesitate to
kick back on the comfy Appalachian quilt because gosh don't you think
you deserve it after all

**Medal of Honor to the brave but just about practically
dying Detective Sands who refuses saying**

after all you've been through. And if the baby just happens to turn out
to be,

**"Aw, shucks, Mother Teresa. Here – you deserve this
more than me." The orphaned children cheer. The
cameras flash. The crowd shouts**

if it just so happens that it turns out to be Bob Sanders, do not be shy
about introducing yourself

**"Bob Sanders! Bob Sanders! Bob Sanders!"**

he is crying pick him up

       **shouting "Bobbie-Bob-Bob!"**

lift him up

       **as they lift him up**

carry him off

       **on their shoulders**

to take him

       **raise him**

home with you

       **up saying**

raise him up

       **Bobbie oh Bobbie sweet baby a baby**

as your

       **of my**

very

       **very**

very

       **own.**

*Bob Sanders* appeared originally in American Writer's Review

Winner - American Writer's Review 2020 Short Story Contest

American Writers Review 2020 (San Fedele Press) Paperback – June 17, 2020

# WILD HORSES
by Nicholas Michael Reeves

*Strange, I know,*
*how sometimes*
*I think of you all,*

*unbridled, out there*
*in the great wide open.*

*No white-cross fence framing*
*God's green earth.*

*Once upon a time, wrote*
*McCarthy, there were woods*
*no one owned.*

*He has a way of nailing*
*our hopes to a cross*
*and resurrecting them.*

*One such hope*
*are you wild horses,*
*pretty enough*

*to make me cry tonight*
*as I whisper*
*wild horses, wild horses.*

*In the city, the drunk men*
*bet on your kin*

*and the most beautiful of you,*
*aged and trodden,*

*have a fresh coat of paint*
*on their hooves*
*as they carriage the rich*

*down the promenades.*

*I have looked long into the*
*earths of their eyes.*

*Green, blue,*
*wet, sad,*
*American eyes.*

*And I have thought*
*of you, wild horses.*

*Don't let*
*them get you.*

*Never let them touch*
*your appaloosa bones.*

*Let us hear your*
*neigh only from*
*the other side of*
*nowhere.*

*You see, I need you tonight,*
*in the way I need the stars.*

*I need to know you're out*
*there, feral and untamed.*

*Believe it or not,*
*I used to be one of you,*

*my beating heart*
*no different*
*than your hooves*

*as I galloped across the*
*burnished plains*
*of my youth.*

*Ears pressed*
*against the pillow,*
*tonight, I listen for the running.*

*I wonder where*
*the wild in me*
*went, the unruly.*

*If my mind were a*
*horse, I'd win the*
*Kentucky Derby,*
*I tell myself.*

*But once upon a time, all*
*I was, was heart—there were*
*woods in me no one*
*owned.*

*No ghosts*
*in the willows.*

*Only a horse, naked,*
*sipping the moon from a stream.*

*No devil on his back,*
*pulling hard on the reins*
*ready to sorrow me the night.*

# MUGSHOT
by Nicholas Michael Reeves

Greeted this morning
by a highwayman guilty
of looting a trailer
of Texas kine.

Up from the morning paper,
he leers at me, that smug
look of his,

which, I'll confess,
makes me a little jealous
as I drink my sweet coffee.

Imagine a life
whose motto was
to hell with it.

5 feet and 11 inches
of hell and high water,

lugging cattle through
the boondocks without
an inkling of a plan,

Texas itself for a nose,
stars of Dallas in his eyes.

A tooth somewhere
in there.

This is a man who refers to
God as the man upstairs,
whose chapel is a saloon.

A man who – if he
ever read Whitman –
would laugh

in his claim that
he was one of
the roughs.

I want to take
a swim through those
40-proof veins

that yellow those
moonshine eyes

I know are there
behind the
black and white
veil of the *Tribune*.

Wash me with
that grease rag of
thinning hair, that tattered
flag of a dying country,
I want to say,

and let's hang
this up in in the
National Gallery
in the wing of portraits.

This every day, American
Mona Lisa,

with a look as obscure
as hers, sly, stark, cunning.

Cornfed, blue collar,
uphill both ways glory.

That is the cheek
his mother used to kiss,
one might whisper,
in a museum voice.

And yes, that is his father
peering out his swollen eye,

through the jailer's lens
into all of Americana,

reminding us
of the many forms of
freedom.

All the day long,
I haven't shaken his gaze.

In the evening, dusk
weeping through the
bathroom blinds,

I saw the prisoner
in the mirror.

as he stared back
into the eyes of the guard.

I ran my hands through
the cold water as if
in search of a key.

And wished I were,
for a moment, a lone
cowboy,

a heathen,
.38 caliber,
yellow tooth
of a man

who slept like
a baby through
the night.

# SIX SEEDS FOR PERSEPHONE
by Gabriel McLeod

---

The sun's rays ignite the grass into golden peaks of fire

Crystalline dew pearls pop open, tiny tears roll down stalks of green

Mourning Doves and Whippoorwills take turns in their songs to one another

Cicadas continue their symphonies from the night before

While the remains of the Moon enter Pisces and obscurities

I step outside of the dark and bathe myself in the grateful apologies of sunrise robes

Like Hades in a fugacious gentle light

Tossing coffee grounds into the yard

Dutiful mourning this beautiful morning

Hard to ignore the longing of belonging

Sometimes a lone wolf doesn't need the night to howl

It is time for Persephone to return to the Underworld

Six seeds it took to bring her to Six Months of Darkness

But I like to think there was love in their opposite attraction along the way

The day's heat threatens to consume us

With the sweat of a memory, we cannot escape

But the night grows closer and cooler each day by minutes

Soon the darkness will reign again

And match the shade of me I don't allow others to see

And I shall sing my song while the Dead sing along

And there I'll be once again with a cloven hooved and crooked fanged smile

Holding my own seeds, squinting out into the light

Waiting for someone to be brave enough to take my hand

For just a little while longer

# MOMENT DURING A STORM
## by Gabriel McLeod

Pondering the palate complexity of the last Cool Ranch Dorito
By candle light in the dark kitchen
As the tropical storm rolls in and lashes against the windows
While my cat companion sits close besides me making eye contact.
We both slow double blink simultaneously
In appreciation for one another.
The roof sounds like the thundering of hooves,
Spilled paint dries on the tiles and my arms
As I stand in the corner, Anxiety anchored in place
Fearful to move less I disrupt the balance of this Universe,
My phone textless black for days on end.
My lucky pen lays upon a python nest of pages of prose
Hungry for order, for meaning, for completion.
Black inked fingertips stroke a thirsty beard.
The storm will wash the acorns from the trees and
Will wash the night a cooler shade of obsidian
Into the fleeting feel of Florida Fall
And for a moment the temperature will bring a post card from the past,
Back when October was fun.
Memories of easier times, of masks, and of rhymes.
Decorations lay await in the attic and the television
Falls back asleep for spending too long on pause.
The streets run like dozens of wet black otters
And I can't help to worry about the bats in the trees,
The tiny birds in the branches,
The pumpkins in the patches,
Empty pail trick or treaters,
The lonely, the lost, the lovelorn.
I look back down at my cat companion,
And he looks up at me and asks, if I am okay with "Meow?"
And I reply, "I will be in a little while."

# AUTHOR FOCUS

WITH ALAN SINCIC AND NICHOLAS MICHAEL REEVES

# "Alan and Cole"

Storyteller Journal exists to not only serve the writer as an individual, but also to honor the invaluable community found between writers as they share their stories, experiences, ideas, struggles, and aspirations. This issue's Author Focus celebrates Alan Sincic and Nicholas Michael Reeves (known as "Cole" to everyone he meets), two writers whose paths crossed at a local coffee shop. From this meeting, a wonderful bond of friendship and camaraderie has formed over the years. Alan and Cole, at different stages of their respective writing careers, together exemplify what the writing community is at its best. Recently, we had the opportunity to catch up with each of them individually to gain some insight into their writing experiences as well as the friendship the two have forged over the years.

## Interview with Alan Sincic

**What advice would you give to somebody who is beginning their journey into the arts?**

There are those who say that, in order to be a great artist (a *visionary* the term they use), you need to explore "altered states of consciousness" – drink or drugs or dangerous escapades out beyond the border of civilized society. They celebrate the tortured genius. I understand the dramatic appeal – Van Gogh with his bloody ear, what a great bio-pic – but I have always felt that we're far too eager to embrace a logical fallacy here. Correlation is not causation. Hemingway and Woolf had turbulent lives that ended in suicide, but that turbulence is not what makes their writing memorable. In the end, what makes a writer great (or not so great) is their facility with words. Yes, life can be hell, and certainly everything you experience can serve the story, but – when all is said and done – you do your best work when you're sober and sane. I'm with Flannery O'Connor here: *Anybody who has survived his childhood has enough information about life to last him the rest of his days.*

**What advice would you give to somebody who has already been writing for some time?**

If you've been writing long enough, you've learned to be wary of would-be mentors. So call this an observation, an offhand remark from one ink-stained wretch to another. Do what you can to preserve that sense of wonder you had when you were a child. It's all too easy for people who are clever with words to slap a label on every mystery, then spend the rest of their lives arguing about the label. The sun is not a curvature in the space/time continuum. The sun is a ball of fire.

**How do you feel the future of writing will be affected by AI, in light of how quickly it is developing and being utilized in the arts?**

It's a bit like the question they asked painters at the advent of photography, or photographers in the era of the cell phone. If you're out there selling a copy of what already exists, there's no way that you can compete with a machine. Nor would you want to.

Which is why, when the machines arrived, the folks who'd been crafting faithful copies of functional items – the potters and the weavers and the smithies – either moved on to other endeavors, or clamored onto higher ground to lay claim to the mantel *artist*. Which makes a lot of sense. We have no heroic John Henry stories of a scrivener in a head-to-head battle with a xerox machine. Why? Because a scrivener is little more than an automaton. An artist, on the other hand – a literary artist – pours the whole of himself into every page he writes. If you think of a work of art as a re-creation of the cosmos as seen through the eyes of a fellow participant – a window into and through the mind of another – then art is, by definition, personal.

Why does this matter? Because, for good or for ill, we are each of us a cosmos unto ourselves – a singularity. Which sounds awesome until you realize (a) you are the only inhabitant in this little goldfish bowl of the brain, (b) you are surrounded by other singularities equally imprisoned, and (c) we've all been dropped into a much larger cosmos over which we have little control. Think of all those mornings you wake with a shock of discovery. *I am not God. The world does not obey me.*

What a boon to the spirit then to visit, now and again, a poem or a story or a novel hand-crafted by a fellow prisoner, a little pocket cosmos over which you exercise – open, close, pause, repeat – a godlike power to explore at will. In the act of reading, we commune with the mind of another. I'm less alone when I encounter, on the page, another I.

Where does AI come in? Well, what is AI? AI is a chorus, an amalgam of a billion voices. Not much consolation when what I'm yearning to hear is the voice of another loner, like me.

**What was it that made you decide to start writing?**

Let me go way back here, long before I could even hold a pencil. I'm safe on my mother's lap, her arms around me. The object in our hands – the big volume of Childcraft that comes with the set of World Book Encyclopedias on the shelf – seems to possess a power of its own that travels, like gravity or magnetism, through the invisible air. It sounds out – the words, they sound out -- not from the painting on the page, or the binding, or the red leather bookmark with the embossment of the bear claw in the foil of gold, but, as if by magic, from out the very center of my mother's body. Nursery rhymes and stories all buzzing with danger – the witch in Hansel and Gretel, the wolf in Little Red Riding Hood, the Jabberwock. I can feel the hum – my little body a sounding board – even before the syllables all round up into shape. *Once upon a time...*

**How do you get yourself through a period of writer's block?**

If you assume that you need to be in a writing mood to write, then woe betide. I have to keep reminding myself that no, I am not a seer, a pipe for the gods to play through. I'm a craftsman. An architect some of the time, sure, but much of the time, a simple bricklayer, one word at a time. There's always a task at hand. After all, this whole business of assembling sentences is so devious, so hypnotically intricate, you can walk up to any pile or stack or rubble of words and set to work. Many times I begin by fixing things – sharpen the image, quicken the rhythm, untangle the syntax – only to find in the end that, without even realizing it, I've broken new ground. Maybe not a cathedral, okay, but look at that bed of mortar there where the stretcher and the header meet! Not so bad for a day's work.

**How has your time on the stage impacted your perspective on the world at large, and writing in particular?**

It got me to thinking about what the stage and the page have in common. Playwrights economize their words, set designers their materials, actors their action. Unlike the moviemaker, for example, who sweeps everything — from the Himalayas to the dimple on the grain of pollen — into the eye of the camera, the set designer *sifts*. From out the avalanche plucks the items — and only those items — that serve the story. The shadow of a windmill conjures a prairie. In a billow of fabric the swell of the sea. In the palm of his hand Hamlet lifts the skull of Yorick. *Alas...*

It's amazing, our ability to pick up on a simple visual cue. The moment we see the set, we complete the picture -- instantaneously fill in the missing pieces. It's that same bit of evolutionary engineering that gave our apey ancestors an edge in the battle for survival. *Look. Twitching up top the shrubbery there. Little black-and-orange strip of fuzzy rope that — Tiger! Run! It's a tiger!*

Writers practice the same bit of wizardry, but with even less to build on. No flesh-and-blood actor. No set. No sound. No lights. Nothing but marks on the page that stand for syllables of air. Out of a million possibilities, we pick the one gesture that reveals character. The chit-chat we sharpen to swordplay. Tuck a decade of battle into a parenthetical aside (*I came, I saw, I conquered*). Not that everybody has to play the minimalist, like Emily Dickenson with her poems no bigger than a doily. It simply means that every word is there for a reason. After all, when you think of Queequeg and Ahab and the whale – the universe he managed to cram between the covers of a book -- Melville was wonderfully succinct.

**What are some unexpected challenges you've encountered in your career thus far, and what advice would you give to new writers as they encounter them?**

There's a temptation to daydream that when you finally -- after arduous effort -- write something really good, readers will, like bees to the bloom, magically gather. Good luck with that. But rather than talk about how difficult it is compete in the somewhat chaotic marketplace today – plenty of articles about the world of publishing – I think it's worthwhile to ask what nudges any of us to write in the first place. For those who write for the money and the fame – for whom writing is the means to that end – the only relevant question is *what does the market say?* I wish them well, and among them are some good writers, but for those of us driven by other desires, who wouldn't turn down the Maserati if offered, but who'd continue to write even if it led to a life of Ramen dinners and rattle-trap cars, what are we hoping to achieve? When you take the earthly rewards off the table, the question becomes a spiritual one.

Kafka despaired of an answer but continued to write in spite of the silence. Tolstoy set out to save the world. Gerard Manley Hopkins wrote to glorify the Maker (*The world is charged with the grandeur of God*) even though in the end (typical writer) he declared himself inadequate. Something tells me that, if I'd been around back in the day, some fifteen thousand years ago, when a few oddballs with torches were crawling into the bowels of the earth to airbrush the imprint of their hand on the wall of the cave, I'd be among that cohort of the deranged. Something impels me to make stories that bear the print of my hand, regardless of how impractical or absurd it all seems. Why? Since I believe that there is something more than this life, I can answer, without irony, *God only knows.*

**What advice would you give yourself today?**

Think beyond the moment. Imagine the world one hundred, two hundred years from now. Will what I write today still be worth reading?

**Also, regarding the dynamic between you and Cole, what is the story of how you became acquainted? What is something that you admire in the other's writing?**

If I say *at the coffee shop* you'll think we lead such dull lives we couldn't possibly be real writers, so I'll let you choose your own adventure – on a tramp steamer off the coast of Indonesia, in a brawl with Hemingway out back of a Parisian Bistro, selling encyclopedias door-to-door in Flannery O'Connor's hometown. Go for it.

As for the writing, we both admire (for example) the poetry of Billy Collins, in particular the way he conjures up a speaking voice that echoes everyday conversation, or lands on metaphors that capture – in a few choice words – the flavor of a scene or a moment or a mood. It's no surprise then I like the way Cole, in his poetry and prose, operates in much the same way: a voice that's vernacular and, at the same time, witty and playful and deft. The poetry percolates up into the prose.

**What are you working on now? Tell us a little about it, what makes it important for you to share?**

Go to alansincic.com for links and a full accounting. Recent online publications include a nonfiction piece (*The Greyhound*) at *The Plentitudes*, a couple of stories (*Eva* and *Mend*) at *Terrain.org*, a sci-fi story (*One Shot Beetle*) at *Hunger Mountain*, and a comic/satirical piece (*Congratulations*) at *Azure*. Upcoming in print: short story *The Winners* in New Ohio Review, short story *Roger Babson* in *The Florida Review*, short story *Potato Boy* in *Orison's Best Spiritual Literature Anthology*, and novel chapter *The God Of The Gator* in *The Thomas Wolfe Review*.

# Interview with Nicholas Michael Reeves

**What was it that made you decide to start writing?**

Books. Lemony Snicket put a fire in me. The library fed it. I had 274.6 Accelerated Reader points in 2nd grade, edging out Connor Song (I miss you, Connor) by eight points. As I fell in love with books, I couldn't help but to write. It's that simple.

**How do you get yourself through a period of writer's block?**

I edit. If I can't think of new ideas, I bog through my slew of old drafts. If that doesn't work, I research. Research is contingent on what I'm writing. My search history could get me twenty-to-life, depending on the weather. No joke. Another writer's block cure is reading. It's impossible to read and not get ideas (ideas are like rabbits). However, it's rare I'm blocked. Burnout is my demise. For all of writing's mystique and allure, it (at least for me) is taxing, gut-wrenching, and at times quite brutal. So it's essential I step away from my work from time to time. To see the forest for the trees. To live. When I'm burnt out, I play piano, go on a drive, watch terrible television, and remind myself that self-expression is (slightly) overrated. What I put on the page isn't me. I tell myself this because writing is so easy to worship. It feels like a mirror, and first drafts are ugly. It's when I step back from my writing and write less that I actually write more. Crazy.

**How do you feel the future of writing will be affected by AI, in light of how quickly it is developing and being utilized in the arts?**

Someone once said our books will soon read us as we read them. eReaders will one day inform AI of our heartbeats, and what "got" us as we flicked the pixelated page. The more we give ourselves to technology, the quicker we can expect to become its product testing animals. This might sound cynical. Perhaps it is. But. As a culture, we get the books we deserve. If the populace is satisfied with shallow, robot-written, banal "literature," that's what will sell. What did Bradbury say, you don't have to burn books to destroy a culture, just get people to quit reading them. My crystal ball is a bit foggy, but this is bad news for literary-minded writers. So yes, AI's effect on the book-biz nauseates me. Why? Because writing, at least to me, is flesh made word. If we let AI win, it means we are admitting we don't need each other's stories. Isn't that terrifying?

**What advice would you give to somebody who is beginning their journey into the arts?**

First, fall in love with the craft. It's love that brings us back to the typewriter, easel, piano, etc. Second, be patient. It's tempting to think that because you have some refined taste in art, you can duplicate that art. But the hard truth is—it can take us a lifetime to become the artist we want to become. Perhaps it should. Third: remember, if you worship art, you'll never feel good enough. I'll paraphrase David

Foster Wallace. If you worship being rich, you'll always feel poor. If you worship being sexy, you'll always be ugly. If you define yourself by the reception of your art, you'll disappointed. There are people I know that love *Twilight*. There are people I know that couldn't finish *The Great Gatsby*. So don't take rejection personally. You'll find your audience.

**What advice would you give to somebody who has already been writing for some time?**

Quit trying to be the writers you love. You make a really shitty J.D. Salinger, my friend. But damn, do you make a beautiful you.

**What advice would you give yourself today?**

You make a really shitty J.D. Salinger, Nicholas Reeves. But you make a beautiful you. Haha, I kid. But not really. My advice to me: Don't confuse motion with progress. Odd advice, but I'm been preaching it to myself. I need to plan more. Free-writing is critical, yes. But once you have your idea, outlining is integral to creating something cohesive, taut. This is what I'd tell me, not anyone else. Some folks free write their way into brilliance. Me? I've written just about every day for a decade. A lot of motion... but to where? My grandmother always says "slow down, you'll get there faster." Good ol' Wanda Sue. I think slowing down is a revolution, especially in context of AI, hustle-culture, etc. Stillness births form. Without form, you can't finish anything. Slow down Nicholas, I tell me. You'll get there faster.

**Also, regarding the dynamic between you and Alan, what is the story of how you became acquainted?**

For six months, I watched Alan sip his coffee and perform autopsies on old manuscripts with the bloody scalpel of an old Bic. "Are you a writer?" I asked him. He smiled. He didn't have to say yes. Now we see each other 3-5 times a week. I try not to fanboy, but he is a hero to me. He's written hard for longer than I've been alive. It's inspiring.

**What is something that you admire in the other's writing?**

I admire Alan's theatricality and experimental bent. If I sampled a hundred award-winning pieces, I could pick Alan's out of the bunch. Reading him, you know he relishes language, truly delights in wordplay, and would choose words over dinner. All that to say: he's a poet. A master of the craft.

**What are you working on now? Tell us a little about it, what makes it important for you to share?**

I'm working on finding an agent for my last novel, *Letters to the Dead* (*LTTD*), as well as a coming-of-age novel called *The Fire We Started*. *LTTD* follows the life of Clifton Henry Ross III in letters he writes to beloved writers and painters. The novel begins in the back of a high school lunchroom in rural 1960s Kansas, when fifteen year-old Clifton writes J.D. Salinger a letter. Five decades and 60,000 words later, Clifton writes his last letter to Harper Lee. *LTTD* means a lot to me because it's a book for bibliophiles. A book that celebrates the power of literature. *The Fire We Started* follows a trio of seventeen year-old boys who accidentally start a forest fire that leads to the death of a teacher from their high school. No one knows they started it. But they do. Can they live with themselves? Should they confess? What will happen if they do? Worse, what will happen if they don't? This novel implores the big questions. That's what writing's all about.

**A specific additional question for you is, what is some guidance or advice that Alan has given you which has been especially helpful?**

Alan once told me I'd the heart of a poet. Encouragement is its own sort of guidance, a launching pad if you will. I carry those words around like some lucky coins. Alan also told me there's stuff he wrote thirty years ago that he is still editing today. This has taught me not to hurry. To keep at it. To give things time. Slow down, Nicholas. You'll get there faster.

**I understand your next novel is a coming of age story. Do you have any moments in your life which you consider to be a distinct coming of age moment?**

Too many. Touching my father's throat tumor while sharing a few beers under a late September moon. Accidentally setting a forest on fire when I was fifteen. Putting the dog down. Saying my last words to my great aunt from 754 miles away, because Covid. Backtrack to high school. A good friend of mine was stabbed to death in a drug deal. Jump to college: Three suicides haunted our small campus one autumn. Jump three years. Sitting in a conference room at "a dream job," feeling like only *Fight Club* could set me free. Geez, this is depressing. Let me say some good ones. Driving around, singing Zeppelin, The Killers, and Relient K with your best friends. Or how about falling in love with my wife. Looking at her every day, knowing—if we grow old together—we'll never grow old.

**What is it which draws you to this theme?**

We are always coming of age. That's my first draw towards the bildungsroman. The second— this theme breaks down all genre barriers. We can't talk about what it means to grow up, or grow old, without addressing how education, politics, history, sexuality, romance, religion, sociology, etc., affect our lives. As such, there is no other genre that gets confronts the big questions so deliberately, with such sheer provocation. They are usually character-driven, nostalgia-overdoses that both simultaneously celebrate life and cut through the world's newest bullshit. They say things most people would be too scared to. They are mirrors that tell us we aren't alone. They show us how love, friendship, and truth stand the test of time, change us, and give us hope.

# GARDEN
THEATRE

## 2023-2024
## BROADWAY ON PLANT SERIES

PRESENTED BY
GARDEN
THEATRE

PRODUCED BY
VICTORY

Jessica Huckabey
THEATRICALS

· AN APPALACHIAN CHRISTMAS TALE ·

By DJ Salisbury
Arrangements by Larry Moore

**WORLD PREMIERE!**

## ON STAGE THROUGH DEC 23

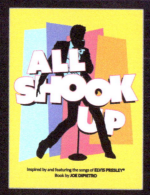

Inspired by and featuring the songs of ELVIS PRESLEY®
Book by JOE DIPIETRO

### FEB 16 - MAR 10          ### APR 26 - MAY 19

## TICKETS ON SALE NOW! GARDENTHEATRE.ORG

SUPPORTED IN PART BY

Arts & Cultural Affairs

Florida ARTS & CULTURE

UNITED ARTS
CENTRAL FLORIDA

VISIT OUR WEBSITE:

# GARDEN THEATRE

## Our History

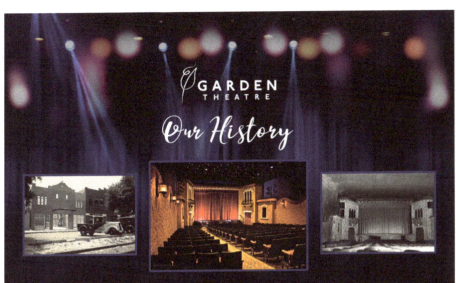

Originally built in 1935 as a single-screen cinema, Garden Theatre was the first in Central Florida built for "talkies," and was a gathering place for locals to watch the latest newsreels and films of the day. Constructed in the Mediterranean Revival style, the interior of the theatre was modeled after a Spanish courtyard with "Romeo and Juliet" balconies, Spanish tile roof, and a dark blue ceiling resplendent with "stars." The theatre underwent several renovations until closing in 1963. Soon after, the interior was completely removed and the sloped floor was covered with cement to level the surface to be used by Pounds Motor Company.

Through the tireless efforts of the Winter Garden Heritage Foundation and the Roper Family, the restored theatre reopened in February 2008. By restoring its architectural charm and re-introducing well-loved family programming as well as bringing innovative and lesser-known works to the stage, the Garden has been instrumental in the revitalization of the downtown historic district.

In the many seasons since, this cultural performing arts center has welcomed thousands of patrons through its doors to enjoy live plays, concerts, movies, dance events, Broadway talent, and educational opportunities.

160 W Plant St | Winter Garden FL | gardentheatre.org

# THE HAWAIIAN CLUB

by Alan Sincic

The neighbors showed up when they heard that I was going to be preparing dinner for the Hawaiian Club. It was going to be just like a Luau but slightly different so that they (the Hawaiian Club) would see that I was no virgin when it came to tropical entertainments. When they (the neighbors) first appeared, I was out in the backyard in my lime-green wetsuit, eating a mango salad and weaving palmetto leaves into a set of placemats. I could hear the whispering as they pressed their faces up against the chain link fence. Some of them had binoculars. Some of them were on the shoulders of the others.

If you want to get into the Hawaiian Club you cannot sit on the sidewalk and whimper. Stop whimpering. Get up off the sidewalk. Here is the toothbrush, here – brush your teeth. If you want to get into the Hawaiian Club you are going to have to put on some clothes.

I add salt water to the aquarium and paint a surfers' stripe down the middle of the ironing board. I throw my biography of Captain James Cook into the blender and add some coconut milk and punch-flavored Kool-Aid. I string together the empty Kool-Aid packages to make an attractive Hawaiian lei.

The difference between a regular pineapple and a Hawaiian club pineapple is that the only kind of pineapple that they will sell you is a regular pineapple. The regular pineapple it tastes like pineapple, but when you eat it there is a syrup that dribbles down the side of your mouth and when you try to wipe your mouth it dribbles down the length of your arms and the hairs on your arm stick to our skin and when you stick your arm under the faucet the water zips down the bones of your wrist to the bones of your elbow and dribbles down onto the crotch of your white khaki dancing shorts and in walks the pretty girl and the meaning of this big yellow blotch of pineapple syrup is that in the eyes of the members of the Hawaiian Club you are no longer the sexually attractive being that at one time you promised to be.

I cannot afford to appear too closely identified with the regular people, no, but neither can I adopt too Hawaiian a tone in my dealings with them. Congeniality. That's the word. That's what the word is. And no doubt, there is no doubt that if you could meet the members of the Hawaiian Club – even just once – then it is certain that they would want you to become a member of the Hawaiian Club. But how could this be possible? If they lived in the place that you live in, if they ate the snacks that you left in your fridge for them or slept in the cot that you made for them or drank the drink that you ordered for them, yes, but they do not. They do not live in the place that you live. The place that you live in does not have the proper Hawaiian atmosphere.

The Hawaiian Club will be arriving at 6pm and it is already 5:55pm. I hurry back to the bedroom to strip off my clothes and to cover my body with coconut oil and even though when I put my clothes back on again they will not know what I have done, I feel pleased for myself that I have done it and that in a sense there is a part of this island of Hawaii that I carry with me on the secret island of my own individual skin.

Eight p.m., and the big oak in the front yard is filled with neighbors. I can hear the rap-rap of their cameras against the bark as they climb higher. They rain down such encouragement upon me that I am ashamed to explain to them what I know about photography: they will be too far away from the Hawaiian Club to get a clear shot, it will be too dark for their tiny flashbulbs to have any effect, the members of the Hawaiian Club will be moving too rapidly to be captured by a ten-dollar instamatic. Even in broad daylight and at close range there are no clear pictures of the members of the Hawaiian Club. Although I explain that this is because of the vigorous personalities of the Hawaiian Club members, and although I do not want to disappoint them (the neighbors), I know in my heart that Hawaiian Club members are not recognized because they do not want to be recognized. At the last possible second the expression on their face will suddenly evaporate into the friendly vagueness of a chummy vacuum cleaner salesman who smiles at you when you open the belly of the vacuum cleaner to show him the seven detachable attachments that belong on the outside of the belly and explain that in some sort of frenzy of cleanliness your wonder vacuum has devoured itself and he smiles at you and nods as if you were a long distance operator from Venezuela trying to connect him in an incomprehensible tongue to a person that he has never heard of before.

If just anybody could get into the Hawaiian Club then it would no longer be the Hawaiian Club. The people who cannot get into the Hawaiian Club are the Pacific Ocean and the Hawaiian Club is the island of Oahu. The front door of the Hawaiian Club is like the beach at Malibu where the Pacific Ocean is trying to climb up onto the island and it is slipping back down into itself and climbing back up again and it is like some sort of sexual thing that is happening and the sound of the big blue ocean banging up against the white beach walls of the Hawaiian Club is a musical sound inside of the ears of the members of the Hawaiian Club.

The wild boar has escaped again and is rummaging through the sugar cane. Again my imperfections pursue me. Already the Hawaiian Club should be feasting on this meal that I have raised from birth for just this occasion, but I am a weakling, I cannot bring myself to roast my little buddy, my confidant, my confessor, my friend.

9:42pm. Sound of drums in the distance. We investigate the source.

9:47pm. Wilma Fredricks has stolen my set of bongos and is instructing her son Bobby in their proper use. I give Bobby a dollar.

I lay the bamboo poles round the perimeter, out yonder by the parrot cages at the foot of the drive.

> hammock
> Polynesian manhood ritual
> Don Ho Records
> conch shells
> Wah-heeni
> Tonka torches
> the flaming baton dance, the hula, the limbo
> Parrot
> grass skirt
> signal flares

11pm. The Mai-Tais are melting. I break out the emergency supplies and festoon the lawn with hibiscus blossoms and chunklets of coconut. Arrival of the Indiana Highway Patrol. There has been some sort of misunderstanding about the roadblock. I show them the diagram etc. Explain etc.

The neighbors refuse to leave, so I invite them in. We wait.

Dawn. The plume of a jet across the sun's red face. Exhilaration and relief. No word from the Hawaiian Club. No sign. No apparition.

In the chill we sit, huddle for warmth, eat the baloney – island style, with our bare hands – and pass the canteen of ceremonial papaya and coconut milk. From out the empty blue, from a way off over yonder, from over the curve of the earth, a breath to bind us all together.

The wild boar settles beside me. Aloha. Between my bare feet he shuffles his head, and with the snout he tickles me, and in the heat of the breath and the spring of the bristle a promise of a day to come, of a day of a size, of a someday. Aloha, amigo. Aloha.

*The Hawaiian Club* was originally published by Sterling Clack Clack (J. New Books)

Winner — Sterling Clack Clack Fiction Contest April 2021

Finalist – 2019 Barry Hannah Prize In Fiction Yalobusha Review

Short Listed — 2020 Gulf Stream Summer Fiction Contest

# PARAPET
### by Vanessa Frances

## *Laura saw daylight for the first time from the back of a cop car*

She'd seen it coming as they rounded the last corner of the tunnel, the fully illuminated road spilling in front of her with impossible depth. The car tumbled forward, light spreading out in front of them at full volume, absorbing the rest of the darkness until Laura forgot it had ever been there at all.

She pushed her head against the cool glass of the window, straining against her cuffed wrists. In the light, the road spilled on forever, rolling around the mountains she'd loved her whole life, illuminated for the first time in her twenty-three years on Earth. It felt like a dream, perceiving the world as intended through smaller pupils and realizing the distance between the hills and the sky she'd always known couldn't possibly be true, only a gap in perception.

"You might want to close your eyes," the officer tapped on the glass separation. "Some people can't handle it." He had slipped on dark sunglasses just as they exited the tunnel completely.

Laura's eyes flickered between the intense green of the trees, a richness that was impossible to observe in the low light of dusk and the sunlight itself at its noontime strength, impossibly bright. She felt the ache in her eyes immediately, squinting but afraid of what she'd miss if she closed her eyes. She blinked open and closed until she took a deep breath and allowed herself to look up.

The sky was a rich and impossible blue, something she'd never known.

Her friends had always sworn it was green.

And she'd believed them.

*What other frame of reference did she have?*

A feeling of excitement built in her chest about reporting the insight back to her friends, who she knew were most definitely still asleep at this hour. None of them could imagine the night she'd had, but especially not this. There was no way to explain *all* of this.

What would they think of her trying to explain the richness in the woods you couldn't see in the dark? Or a description of the height of the mountain twofold to what they'd always guessed it to be?

*And the sky-*

Laura strained against the window, trying to take in every last inch of blue, pushing herself up on her constrained wrists. Her stomach dropped.

She wouldn't be able to do that.

She knew, deep down, this would probably be her *first* and *last* time seeing the world with its lights on. There would be no return trip.

The August heat radiated across the ground before them, and Laura felt it coming at her through the glass. This is what a world designed for people that rose and set with the sun looked like: open and spacious, running further than anything you could imagine against the ink-black night sky.

The world before Laura contrasted against the inverted night-centered world created by adaptation to increased temperatures and heat advisories. In the world she was familiar with, working outside was only possible so long as there was no daylight interference. It was a system that preserved out-of-date ways of living by separating man from light.

This scene expanding in front of her was one that anyone not a public servant hadn't seen in nearly sixty years, much longer than Laura had been alive.

The government determined that turning everyone nocturnal was much

> **" Her parents painted such a frightening world where people and the planet were disregarded enough that living without light was now better than facing it.**

easier than mandating that oil companies, billionaires, and first-world countries cut their emissions. So humans adapted their sleep schedules: Rest from 6 am to 9 pm, work and live your life between 9 pm and 6 am, rinse and repeat. Neighbors commuted together to office jobs at 9 and 10 pm. Children arrived home from school closer to 3 am for a 5 am dinner and news broadcast. Teenage love birds snuck out for dawn first dates to catch the first moments of light before rushing inside before the 8 am curfew. The new normal. In pursuit of something adjacent to survival.

Call it Genetically Modified Evolution.

Laura's parents had lived before inverted sleep schedules and subsidized blackout curtains. They told her stories about the impossible heat of the daytime and the number of people who had died doing their jobs without water breaks or temperature control. Crops failed enough to where all food was grown quietly in labs. Animals perished against the pressure cooker sunlight on these same dark asphalt roads Laura now weaved around. Her parents painted such a frightening world where people and the planet were disregarded enough that living without light was now better than facing it.

So they did just that, creating special glasses, darker curtains, underground housing, special supplements, Vitamin D lamps, and contrived spiritual lore about "the ancient people" that had lived against the sun until it was more believable to catch glimpses of bats than birds. Laura's grandfather had kept a book of stamps from the old days, birds with vibrant colors like red and blue, animals she could only imagine that showed up in her dreams as disfigured, nocturnal, and uncanny versions of what they might be. Her brain had no other way of perceiving it then, what it might be, and not what she imagined.

No picture of the sky, forest, or woods did them justice.

And no streetlight, headlamp, flashlight, or flood light compared to the sun itself.

Seeing the daylight in person made every other light feel like a cheap imitation, children playing creator in trying to dictate the world they perceive. It was so easy to get lost in your perception when you could barely see your hands in front of your face.

Laura's eyes began to burn. Drinking in all the light unfolding before her was too much to swallow. Her eyes squinted shut, aching.

"What did I say?" The officer frowned, looking back at her through the rearview mirror.

"I just want to see it," Laura clenched her eyes. "I'm not doing anything wrong by looking, am I?"

"It's a lot to take in at once," the officer clicked his tongue. "I've had plenty of people have panic attacks in the back of this car coming out of that tunnel, trying to do the same thing you just did."

Laura's throat tightened.

"Not like I'm going to get another opportunity, am I?"

The officer tapped his fingers on the dashboard. Laura followed the sound of his fingers sliding back to the steering wheel, falling silent.

Laura held still, eyes shut, and turned back toward the window. The light was strong enough to come through the skin of her eyes, turning her world a distinct shade of red and pink. Laura could see all the blood vessels from the inside of her eyes, the pulse of blood flowing across her pupil, signs of life she'd never been privy to.

"Come on," she murmured. "Look again."

Her eyes ached but cooperated, and she allowed herself to take in the scenes in front of her much slower than she had initially, pausing incrementally to rest her eyes. The car had rounded another corner and was declining toward the extended road below. Laura rested her head against the window, the glass no longer cool as it had been when they'd first exited the tunnel but growing increasingly hot.

"What's the temperature outside?" Laura leaned down to brush some of the sweat beads pooling on her forehead to the shoulder of her shirt. She'd never felt heat like this before. Even from inside the air-conditioned car, she felt its intensity radiating.

"128 today," the officer replied almost indifferently. "Coolest it's been this week."

"128?" Laura's eyes widened, but she retracted them, taking in too much of the sunlight.

"Mhm. Makes you thankful for the way we live, doesn't it?"

Laura's gaze drifted back toward the rolling scenery, the trees' intense greenery, and the mountain's depth. In the distance, and only momentarily, she spotted a bird with feathers as vibrant blue as the sky, racing out from the covered tree branches towards an exposed hollow. It was more beautiful than any stamp she'd ever seen.

"Maybe," she replied. "Maybe not."

Staring out the window, Laura watched as the bird leaped out of the hollow and flew parallel to the cop car, leaping up above the silver barricade and journeying with them down the final stretch of mountain road before diverting back into the deep wood. Laura studied the bird as it transformed into a distant blue dot for as long as her eyes could take it before she blinked, and it had disappeared completely.

"I've watched enough people die in this heat to know it's safer how we live."

"People die in the dark too."

Looking back inside the car, Laura caught the officer's gaze in the rearview mirror, his eyes concealed behind his glasses, shrouded in darkness.

"I'm sure you know that," Laura clenched her jaw.

It was easier to wrong your neighbor when everyone's waking hours were determined by survival. Those exact schedules made to keep the peace had sewn opportunity for those looking to find it, good, bad, and honest.

The officer scrunched his nose and bit his lip, thinking. She watched as he tapped on the steering wheel again, not breaking her gaze until he turned back towards the road. The car slowed to a halt.

"What's happening?" Laura frowned.

The officer pulled off to the side of the road and parked the car. He exited the driver's seat, walked around to the back where Laura was sitting, and pulled open the door beside her.

The heat hit Laura immediately, the humidity sticking to her skin like hot water poured across her face and neck. For the first time, she took in the man-made world at full force: its three-figure heat, tightening its fingers around her neck.

"Get up," the officer scolded, but Laura sat still.

"UP!" he shouted, slamming his fist on the car's hood. Laura flinched and did as she was told, standing up and letting the sunlight engulf her.

It was overwhelming.

Her whole body burned with intolerance built from a life without actual sunlight. She felt herself sweating immensely, her thirst intensified, and everything, everywhere, was so extraordinarily bright—all of it.

"Are you trying to kill me?" Laura huffed.

"Look at yourself," the officer spat. Laura watched him use the back of his wrist to wipe the sweat off his forehead. He couldn't have been any older than her. That was something she could tell in the light, that they'd been on this Earth for the same amount of time. But where her skin was translucent white, his ventures back and forth underneath the sun had made his skin distinctively darker. She caught a glimpse of pale skin just near the top of his uniform collar.

"Not me," he stepped closer, and Laura instinctively stepped back. " Look at yourself."

Confused, Laura looked down at her feet. Her worn tennis shoes were on top of mismatched socks, one just darker blue than the other. She was so pale, more so than she'd even realized until standing in this light. Her eyes journeyed up her legs to her dark gray shorts and toward her midriff. She squinted again.

Across her middle, stained in lines between her shorts and green shirt, were deep crimson lines, wet and dark. She'd never seen anything like it before. It was so rich that it almost hurt her eyes as much as the light just beyond the tunnel had.

Her eyes continued to make their way up the rest of her clothes, and the crimson stripes ran from her shoulders to just above her hands, getting distinctively darker as the stain grew out toward her wrists but stopping above her spotless hands. It was so bright that looking at it was beginning to make her nauseous. She'd never seen anything like it before.

"What is this?" Laura frowned.

The officer's jaw tightened. "Blood."

Laura's stomach threatened to empty itself at that moment. Her heart pounded in her chest, eyes darting between the officer and the blood on her shirt and shorts, contrasting with her pale, clean wrists and hands. Her eyes shot out across the dirt toward the officer and she saw the same matching shade of crimson sprinkled across the bottom hem of his pants and shoes.

Now that she was looking at the blood, Laura could *smell it;* rich with iron and salt.

Everything she had tried to forget in the last seven hours came racing back into her head. The fight. The thrown insults. Her sister revealed she'd slept with her husband—the snake-eyed coyness. Laura's hands found her throat and then the boning knife. The aftermath. The vibrant blue and red lights on the cop car against the darkness. The cold water against her hands in the sink, not realizing they weren't the only things that had gotten dirty. The officer's feet confirmed that.

"That can't-" Laura's brain rattled. "I cleaned all of it off before- there's no."

"Amazing what we can't see until there's enough light, huh?" The officer frowned. "The guilt feels real when you see the consequences."

Laura's heart was racing, her brain rattling, but there was no escape from this. Everything was louder in the daylight. Even with her eyes closed, the safety of total darkness was nowhere to be found. The heat intensified her throat, gasping for water as much as air, drowning in all the heaviness pouring into her at once. She leaned over, lurching into the grass, a new shade of green topped off by another from her stomach.

Laura was entirely exposed, all of her. There was nowhere to go.

Nothing to hide from. Nothing worth hiding for.

Her eyes shot open, finding the deep brown of the dirt below her feet, scanning the ground and darting her eyes away from her soiled clothes and up to the sky.

In its full glory, the sky was immaculate. Bluer than the bird she'd seen, bluer than any photograph, but still less blue than her sister's widened eyes as Laura grew close enough to finally appreciate the color. They looked just like her grandfather's had. She wondered if they looked like hers too. She'd never found a way to look.

Staring at the sun made Laura's eyes ache to the point she finally had to look away, clenching them shut and turning back towards the ground. She felt the urge to cry, but her eyes were much too dry for tears, so she settled for choking on the snot as it rolled down the back of her throat.

There was a tap on her shoulder, and the officer reached down and lifted her chin, sliding a pair of dark sunglasses over her closed eyes. Laura blinked, her eyes adjusting to more familiar hues, dampened hues of green and brown, the sky a different shade of blue. She lifted her shoulder to wipe the sweat and snot off her face, feeling the pull of her handcuffs.

The officer touched her head, guiding her back toward the police car. His hand was heavy, insistent. Laura sat back in the seat, looking up in just enough time to see the officer putting another pair of sunglasses over his eyes. He stared at her momentarily, his jaw tightening before his lips melted into a frown.

Squinting up at him, she saw the blue sky in a narrow sliver above her glasses as the officer closed the door.

Laura closed her eyes.

# INCANDESCENT RAGE
by Joe Tankersley

## *The explosion of harsh yellow light nearly blinded Sheila when she opened the apartment door*

She knew immediately what that bastard Kevin had done. One last petty act of childish aggression, literally on his way out the door.

Where had he even found incandescent light bulbs? Much less decided it was worth his time to change out every LED in her apartment.

Leaving him alone in the apartment to pick up his things had been a mistake, but she couldn't imagine sharing the space with him for another minute. Now Sheila was paying the price for trusting him again. She wasn't sure if it was that thought or the harshness of the lights that made her feel dizzy. God, how did anyone ever stand that awful yellow glow?

She steadied herself and considered her options. She could turn all the lights off with the one switch at the door. Sheila had insisted the landlord add the European style master switch when she learned it saved on average 3.5% of the monthly electric usage. That is, if you used it, which Kevin had made a point of never doing.

Trying to find where he had hidden the LED bulbs and replacing them in the dark didn't sound like the best idea. Not to mention having to deal with whatever other unwelcome surprises Kevin had left for her. Instead, she pulled the shade off the retro floor lamp next to the sofa. Three bare bulbs blasted at her. Without thinking, she grabbed the closest one and immediately screamed in pain as the hot bulb seared her fingers.

She rushed to the kitchen and ran precious water over her fingers. In her mind's eye, she saw the spinning dial of her water meter speed up even more. That bastard was going to cost her everything he could before disappearing from her life.

The pain finally subsided. She opened the kitchen drawer where she kept her dish towels. She had to dig through the single use fast-food condiment packages Kevin had squirreled away to find one. Sheila gently patted her blistered fingers dry.

Back in the living room, she used a towel to remove the still hot bulbs from the floor lamp. Emboldened by her success, she attacked the other lamps throughout the apartment. In minutes, the only incandescent bulbs left were the ones blazing like demented suns overhead. Those would have to wait until she had searched the rest of the apartment to see what other environmental traps Kevin had set for her.

Sheila shivered at the thought. No wait, she shivered because now that the apartment was free of artificial heat, she could tell that the AC was running full blast. The jerk had taken a hammer to the smart thermostat and destroyed the limit switch.

"Bastard," Sheila muttered through chattering teeth as she dug through the hall closet for the fuse box. She swung the panel open and flipped off the HVAC without reading the neatly printed labels. No need, as she always turned off the system when she traveled. Just one of the many "quirks" that Kevin had made fun of her about. How had she not seen through him?

They had met six months ago, on Earth Day at Lake Eola Park. Sheila and the other members of the Orlando chapter of Extinction Rebellion had organized a massive die off. Nearly one hundred of them lay in the blistering sun for nearly three hours. All the major streamers had reported on their effort. A semi-famous eco-blogger had even interviewed Sheila.

The Earth Day party lasted long after the demonstration. Sheila and her friends, Jenni and Kate, stayed until the very end. When they finally started the short walk down Central toward their apartments, they were still buzzing from the energy of the day. The street was filled with young people all around the same age. They didn't really pay much attention to the four guys following them, until right in front of the Publix, the guys called out. They were friendly, polite. Kevin did most of the talking. He was tall, with slightly unkempt blonde hair and dreamy blue eyes. Good looking enough that Sheila hadn't minded that he really didn't seem to know much about the day's events. She assumed he was a newbie.

Conversation led to an invitation to stop for drinks at Sheila's favorite wine bar. After sharing a bottle of wine, organic natch, the guys insisted they hit some other bars. One stop became two, then a third before the group ended up in one of the truly scuzzy places on Orange Ave. The kind Sheila and her friends avoided. Despite the stench of antiseptic and heavy metal blaring from distorted speakers, they agreed to one last round. Shots of cheap tequila sparked a passionate make-out session for Sheila and Kevin.

When the lights finally came on at the last call, Kevin hinted he wanted to go home with her. Kate and Jenni quickly intervened. They pulled her out of the bar and into a waiting Uber. The next morning, Sheila nursed her hangover and wrote the night off as nothing more than a fleeting moment of impulsiveness.

If only Kevin hadn't texted her the following weekend. But of course he did, and she accepted his invitation to lunch at her favorite vegan café. By the end of the first month, he had essentially moved in. She told herself that living in a world rushing toward climate Armageddon it was foolish to delay what pleasure she could find.

> **" She took a long swig, let the wine wash away some of the anger bile before opening the cabinet to drop the empty bottle in the recycling bin.**

"Damn." She slammed the fuse box closed and kicked the closet door shut.

The hard click of the AC shutting off filled Sheila with resolve. She was a bad-ass eco-warrior, and no cruel climate-denier was going to get to her. She marched into the bedroom, ready to conquer whatever new challenge he had left.

She collapsed on the bed when she saw the pile of broken wooden hangers on the floor. Hangers that Sheila had discovered at her favorite thrift store. A purchase she had been so proud of as part of her mission to live plastic free. Kevin had left the closet door open so she couldn't miss the row of outfits, also thrifted, carefully hung on brand new colorful plastic hangers. Time for a drink was all Sheila could think in response.

Back in the kitchen, she emptied a half-filled bottle of wine into a tall glass. She took a long swig, let the wine wash away some of the anger bile before opening the cabinet to drop the empty bottle in the recycling bin. The bottle landed with a dull thud in the empty bin. The sound was all wrong. Tomorrow was recycling day, and the bin had been full when she left the apartment earlier. She bent down, pulled the bin out, and found the note. Kevin had scrawled the message in his big, looping handwriting. *Took the GARBAGE out for you.*

They had fought over her insistence that all recyclable items go into the bin. Kevin had argued that it was a hoax. He printed out articles from sketchy websites that claimed the sanitation department dumped everything in the landfill. Sheila had tried to explain that she could only be responsible for her choices. He had accused her of being brainwashed.

It had been their first fight, shortly after he had moved in. She had tried to be reasonable and suggested that since it was her apartment, and he wasn't paying any rent, the least he could do was follow her rules. He agreed and even seemed to try. Sheila was shocked when she discovered that he was bringing plastic soda bottles into the apartment and burying them deep in the garbage can. When she confronted him, he offered some lame excuse and promised to stop. He didn't. Ultimately, she gave up and just went through the trash regularly before recycling day.

Still she had let him stay. Why? She slumped at the kitchen counter and drank her wine. How could she have been so stupid? Another swig of wine and she pulled herself up.

No! She wasn't to blame. He had conned her. At first, he had even tried to convince her he shared her values. Looking back, she should have been suspicious when he always had an excuse for not joining her for marches or chapter meetings.

His kind concerned act didn't last very long. She guessed putting on the con 24 -7 had been more work than he expected. She tried to ignore most of the little slips. She knew how hard it was to live a clean life in a throwaway culture. In some ways, she saw helping him improve as her mission.

Then one day he exploded. Sheila had casually mentioned that he had, for like the umpteenth time, left the lights on when he left the apartment. How frickin hard was it to flip one switch right by the door?

The white-hot intensity of his reaction was terrifying. He screamed and called her hateful names before slamming the door and leaving. When he came back later that night, he crawled into bed next to her but said nothing.

He was gleefully wasteful after that. He would follow her around the apartment to turn on lights she had just turned off. Toss empty beer cans in the trash right in front of her.

By the end of the week, Sheila knew she had to do something. She got up early to fix his favorite breakfast. She even went to the deli down the street and bought him real bacon. The smell of it frying in the pan almost made her gag, but she was determined to give the relationship one last chance. It was nearly noon when he finally came out of the bedroom, shirtless, hair uncombed. The first thing she noticed was the beginning of a beer belly that hung over the waist of his stupid lime green polyester gym shorts. How had she not seen what a complete slob he was? She pasted a cheery smile on her face.

"Morning," she said. "I made us breakfast. Thought we could talk." She slid a plate across the counter.

He inspected the free-range organic eggs sitting next to the two strips of bacon glistening with fat. Then broke out into demented laughter.

"You are so fucking pathetic."

She jumped at the force of his words. "I don't... understand."

That was all it took to launch Kevin into a diatribe that lasted for the next twenty minutes. One he had apparently been waiting to deliver. He explained in painful detail how he and his buds had been trolling for greenies the night they met. He had bet his bros he could get her to sleep with him. After that turned out to be so easy, he upped the ante and bet them he could get her to let him move in. She stood there, mouth open through the entire speech, right up to the moment he announced with a snicker.

"Greenie, it's all been one big con job. And you know why it was so easy? Because fools like you are already brainwashed."

That was when she slapped him as hard as she could and screamed, "Get out of my apartment now!" When he just stood there smirking, she added, "Before I call the police."

He grabbed a slice of bacon, crammed it in his mouth, and headed for the door. Over his shoulder he called out, "yeah you do that and make sure to tell them what a patsy you are."

That was the last time she saw him. After that, they communicated by text to arrange the pickup of his clothes and a few other possessions. She carefully packed the items and left them on the kitchen counter. She arranged for him to come while she was at her weekly Extinction Rebellion meeting. She thought being around friends would help her not obsess about him being in her apartment alone. No way she expected him to be such an ass.

At least the meeting had been a useful distraction. Everyone was excited about the news that someone had broken into the OUC substation in Lake Nona and shorted out half the transformers. Most of the area lost power, including the medical complex.

Sheila's chapter had a firm nonviolence rule, but there were a few people there that night who wanted to celebrate the act. The discussion had turned into a loud and heated debate. Those opposed to acts of violence argued that it only turned public support against them. Michelle, the group's leader, had even suggested that if anyone knew the perpetrators, they had a duty to report them to the police.

As Sheila sat at the table and finished her wine, she googled the substation attack. Scrolled to the bottom of the first article and found what she was looking for. The phone number for the police tip line. She hesitated for a moment, then thought. Hey, just doing what you said, Kev baby, and dialed.

The chatbot on the other end of the line invited her to share her information.

"Yes, I think I know who attacked the substation in Lake Nona. His name is Kevin Bronaugh."

She gave a few more details, but not her name, and hung up.

Looking up from her phone, she squinted into the bare bulb left in the overhead light. Soon she would have to pull out the stepladder and replace it with the soft cool glow of an LED, but for now she let her rage rest in its incandescent glare.

# MEND

## by Alan Sincic

On the mend. It don't amount to much, from overhead, coming in out the clouds, nothing really, the sight of a tent up in the arms of a tree, and nothing but air beneath it -- satchel of canvas surfing the swell -- but you'd be mistaken. Come take a look. On the plank in the crown of the cypress, under the tarp that splits the wind and parries the sun, lies a man all beat to hell. Beat but on the mend. Green again. Grateful, and like any other man who ever lived, a cosmos in the making. So it seemed to GB. Awake or asleep, ragged or spruce, horny or hale or all beat to hell and back again, it don't matter he figured, it's all the same: every day you wake, and poke your nose up out the bedcovers, and discover you ain't dead yet, that day's the day God said *Let there be light*. The first day of creation.

The boy waited, then spoke. "I can get Maggie to bring – "

"You don't tell Maggie nothing. Don't even tell her you seen me."

"She gonna come looking. She knows about the tree-fort."

"Tell her you seen me at the depot. Tell her you seen me – " Barnett pictured himself at the depot, attaché in hand, the brim of the fedora bent to match the curve of the earth. Watched himself whip out a cigar, finger the fob of the pocket watch, the -- what do they call it? -- *fret* at the neck of the fiddle.

"Tell her I was boarding the train. North. Not the local. No. Savannah maybe."

"Savannah?"

"You decide."

The boy was a wonder. Whatever you tell him, he takes it all in, neither believing or disbelieving, and not like he ain't sharp enough to see the difference, but he got him a scale of his own to weigh it, touch it, tell if it's crooked or true. It was Sparrow made him see what Maggie wanted. Not in so many words -- mute as a mushroom, Sparrow -- but in the way he moved. Allowed himself to be carried in the current of the come and the go, to travel in the shadow of Maggie without losing that shadow of his own. Nothing but the pleasure of his company is what the boy give her, and no charge, cheap as a breeze, but that was enough. No money, no trade, no property? No matter. Not so big on ownership, Maggie.

To Maggie the land was no more than the dirt beneath her feet. Defended her territory same as any other creature of the wild, sure, but to her the land was a field of battle, a room to maneuver in that war of hers against everything and everybody. You travel the land. That's what it's for. To parcel it? Price it? Pay it out by the yard like a length of batting? You'd sooner slip a river in your pocket or carve yourself a slice of air.

No wonder then, when it come to Maggie and Barnett, you got yourself a collision. For Barnett it was always the land. He figured the way to win a gal like Maggie was to gather up a spread of a size to make him a squire, a man to be reckoned with, a citizen true.

Mercy. What a sap.

No you say? Okay. Have it your way. A logical man, okay, but a logic that made him, in the game of love, a fool. He figured inches, feet, yards. Acreage he figured. The imprint of them boots of his too small a claim to carry the day. He pictured himself with a deed in hand to cover the whole of the earth, and the oceans to boot, and the grains of sand by the billion at the border between the two. Everywhere's where he would be. No place to plant a foot without a charge of trespass. Only then would he relent. Surprise her. Give her back, pressed down and running over, the whole of the world she'd – in her stubborn way – always refused before.

And who knows? Maybe today was the day to begin. Begin again. From up top of the tree the territory, the sight of the territory, stirred in him a hope. What with the broke arm and the face all purpled up into a bruise, more like a notion than a hope, but hell. You do what you do, right? When you don't got a breeze you settle for a breath. You can live on a breath. Be grateful. Plenty people don't even got so much as a breath. The boys who beat him? What do they got? Blood is what they got. You whack a pinata you win the prize. But that's it. The all of it.

*But don't they got the truth?* you say, say you. Sure they got the truth -- from out the vasty ocean a pincher of salt. A factual. A dead letter of the law is all, and all because – nobody's fault but their own – they don't got the capacity to appreciate the grandeur of the vigorous lie.

\* \* \* \* \* \*

For sure the arm was – below the elbow there – broke. In the binding it swelled. The pain got a rhythm, a throb to the beat of the heart, *greenstick fracture* they call it, as if blood were the same as sap, and flesh the same as wood, and the bone the bole of a tree you break to feed, in the end, a fire.

Never mind. No never mind. *Come back in a week* he said to the boy. *Gimme a week.* They'd nobody find him here, no, not after all the trouble the boy'd taken to hoist him, inch by inch, up the trunk and into the arms of the tree. Here was a place to mend, a here worth a having, where the crown umbrellas up into the sun, snuffs out the branches below, carves out a cavern of green.

The boy poled away, off the bank and down-river. GB pictured the day they decided, him and Sparrow, to conquer the tree. To build 'em a fort. Outside the map is what it was, out in the bed of the river, the cypress, a part of the river but outside the reach of the rod and the chain. *Free and clear* they said, they laughed. *Nobody owns the air!*

Over the summer they'd labored, him and the boy. Into the flesh of the cypress they'd hammered a spike, head-high, another then another, so's to boost the boy up the bare trunk and into the lower branches. Off a broken dock they crow-barred the boards. Upstream they rafted them, and into the shallows and up the tree they hauled them, one after the other, to corduroy out, over the limbs, a platform scabrid as the hide of a gator. The pulley was Sparrow's idea. "Like a elevator," he said. "A elevator for ammo." A castle keep is what it was, the treehouse. They rigged a rope to a basket full of provisions and then winched it, hand over hand, up the forty feet or so to the larder they fashioned from the trunk of a steamer.

A helluva climb to be sure, but from up top, from a perch on the four-by-four that shot out beyond the bounds of the platform and into the sun you could see, to the south, when the weather was good, the whole of the grove. The packers. The pickers. Every which way the ladders they pitch up into the plush, the bins that bubble over to speckle the earth, the beekeeper that sets the dogs to bark as he grapples, from out the portable cloud he carries, a jagged chunk of honey. Thick the wind with the scent of the peel of the orange. Sharp on the tongue the salt of the brow. The skin a shiver in the rain.

How they would argue away the hour with a game of *who goes there?* A point for every person you, with your eagle eye, spy. And even now, in the dark, in the moment of recollection, how fierce the color – the copper spout of the still, the red blaze of the robin, the bright geyser of sand the gale, as it rounds the mouth of the quarry, kicks up into the blue. How the boy would babble over the stir of it all, the rattle of the hopper and the roar – faint now at such a distance -- of the pulper. The zig and the zag of the clay path where round and about the tractor rambles, into the green and out again (*There! I told ya, I told ya – there he goes!*) – the clay the color of a Dreamsicle or the heart of a mango or the ember you jar with a poke of the stick.

"I spy," the boy'd say. "Lookee yonder there, the bridge, the fella with the neckerchief, the yellow, there slapping – see? Slapping a horsefly."

"You telling me you can see – "

"Look at him, look. Smacking himself (point, point for me) on the back of the neck."

Point. Point-Set-Match. Silence. Topside the two as they master the province, give it the God's eye, cradle the lake in the palm of the hand, whisper up a wind so's to shoo the cloud away, so's to spy the glint-of-the-razor rail that cleaves the land and divvies the green into buyable portions, so's to hail the fella at the helm of the Jenny there paying out, in a plume of vapor trim as a bead of icing, the word *Jesus*, and so's to hear, off and away, and beyond the reach of the voice, faint as a head of thunder in a build at the brim of the earth, a rumble of dozers and sluice buckets and dredgers.

The whole of the summer they labored to build it. To make it so. To reckon up, at the end of a day, the gain, the keepsake of a day worth a keeping and the cry, come the dusk, of the osprey and the hawk, and the fireflies in a cinder, and the turn of the season, and the moon as it fattens, and the chill air that gives the breath a shape, a heft, a body the color of bone.

\* \* \* \* \* \*

Into the shade he shuffled the cooler, the case of gin, the jugs of water, the mess kit and the jerky and the tin of biscuits. Gathered up under the tarp a basket of gear – the bug spray and the Bowie, the torchlight and the trencher and the rope in a coil. The slop bucket he hung from a length of chain off the end of the platform. The whiskey the boy'd fetched him – bottle from out the hollow of a tree – he swaddled in a strip of gauze. The doc in a bottle. The germ-killer, pain-killer, kissable buddy in the cold of the night. Into the sling it went.

The first two days he drank. This he could do. This he was good at. To an assembly of leaves he spoke. A claim is what it was, the treehouse, a bid to be the boss of a sky bigger than a breath or a billow of smoke, bigger than the blue that binds the earth. Gave the sky a punch. Stirred the air. The invisible swirl of the citrus brushed him on the cheek. God if you could rake it up into a bushel or a bale, a bottle, a brew, the scent of the grove, think of it, just think. Again he felt the ache – it surprised him, all broke as he was – to feel the quick of it, the yen for the place, and the power in the hand to make the place, his the hand, his, the hand of the Maker. Stackable the clouds. Breakable the waves. The blue of the sky and the bully green of the tree.

He licked his knuckle. The split at the ridge. The red furrow down the heel of the hand, where he'd parried the blow of the crowbar. He savored again the uppercut, the counter-punch, the shock of the fist in the face of that bastard. A sight to behold. A sign from on high. Out there somewhere in a shamble off the porch of a shanty, God willing -- dumb cracker with a broke tooth!

Bastard. The bastards. The boys who beat him shoulda been thanking him for the lesson he conveyed. *To see it is to be it* is what he told 'em, and they believed, and in the believing saw – for so long as they believed – a vista magestical and, at the same time, cozy. If he hadn't of sold 'em a deed to a property that don't exist, they never woulda had the pleasure of the picture of that red brick house on the bank of the river with the skiff and the dock and the dog, the chill at the lip of the jug and the bass nipping at the bait and, bobbing up out the water at dawn, that red ball of the sun. Grand is what it was. And ain't that a pleasure in its own right? The picture? And the bonus at the end, right? The righteous pleasure of beating the tar out the fella sold you the picture.

\* \* \* \* \* \*

Sundown. Day three. Careful, like you fold a pastry, into the quilt he rolled, and onto his side, the wad of a towel for a pillow and, up top, the arm in a sling. In the hold at the heart of a cocoon he pictured himself. Fold upon fold the quilt, the tarp, the canopy of green, as if to shield himself from that brute of a moon, that savage assay of the sun. Slept.

> **“ He woke. It was nothing, he figured. Wind is what? Wind is air. And air is what? Air is – put your hand out. Give it a shake. Nothing. Air is nothing.**

Come the night, midnight or so, a gust of wind ripped the canvas off the frame and flung it overboard. You think, when you sleep, the universe shutters the blinds and the planets pause and that flower the sun flutters to a halt. The earth -- the buzz of that little bee -- brakes. The buzzing stops – and why? Because the god of it all sleeps. Say who? You. You there. The center of the universe. That's what we all of us – am I right or am I right? – feel about the world out there on the far side of the lid of the eye.

He woke. It was nothing, he figured. Wind is what? Wind is air. And air is what? Air is – put your hand out. Give it a shake. Nothing. Air is nothing. And the sky was empty. Not a cloud. Not a spit of rain. The moon is all, the *Maggie moon* he called it on account of the promise he made to buy it for her. She laughed. Smacked him on the head. "Like you got a grift enough to win you a planet."

"A planet's too much for you to handle, Maggie. A moon's the fit for a gal like you, all bitter and chilly and bare."

The moon looked on. The deck swayed in the grip of the nothing, rode up and then down like a ship on a swell. From a ways off, upriver, the timber roared. In a race it came, the roar. The nothing swept away the sleeping bags, the clothes, the cooler with the food. Into a gap in the planking he thrust the one good hand. Anchored himself. He knew the floor would hold (four-by-fours bolted at the branch) so he did what the tree did. Rode the wind. Starboard or port. Up or down.

As if to make his body a smaller target he curled up into a ball, the broken arm in the center, the eggshell of the hip and the shoulder and the back of the skull a shield. To die here, impaled on the knee of a cypress or -- head-first -- post-holed into the muck? Talk about a outrage. If it were lightening. He could abide by that. That he could abide. A meteor. *Struck By A Meteor: GB Bites The Dust* -- every damn diner, barroom, breakfast table set to buzzin with news of his demise. It ain't too much to ask, is it, of God, if there is a God? To die in a manner marvelous? Plucked by a twister and dropped, downriver, onto the javelin head of a steeple; bazooka-ed up into orbit from out the mouth of a volcano; flash-frozen in a hollow at the heart of a tree?

The steamer trunk slid to the lip of the platform. Tremored. Over the side it went. Struck the bone of wood at the base of the tree. Splinters. The rain that followed beat the branch above him, the plank that held him, the bare shoulders he bowed upwards to parry the blow. Keen to shatter the earth, that's what the rain was about, what its intent was, but the earth bullied on. The body of the tree battled. The rope handle of the crate he hooked with his foot. Gave it a tug. The bottles pinged. The gin quivered. He pictured the boys in a crowd around him at the end of the bar, him bragging how he beat the odds, broke a twister, a flood, a fusillade of locust and brimstone and hail.

The branch gave way but he was ready. Into the crotch of the tree hauled himself. Thunder he thought it was, at first, the shipwreck of the deck come crashing, come – leaf and limb, spike-spar-plank – avalanching down.

He licked the blood off the palm of his hand. Cradled the broken arm. From outta the sea the salt in the blood, that's what they say. He coulda been a fish. A bear. A vulture. Who's to say? God took it upon Himself to make a *Barnett* is what He did, the bastard and then bam. Goodbye. Up here. Left him. In the trunk of the tree. Busted. Broke. Bereft. That would be the word. Bereft.

So be it. Let the timber howl and the granite buckle and the clouds mountain up to bury the earth. By the power of the liquor and the flame of the spirit of grift ever eternal within, he vowed that he would – yea verily, and let the heavens be damned – master the moment. He tucked himself, butt first, into the bole of the tree. Bowed his head. Shut his eyes. Bye and bye the body wrestled, rocked him, pulled him into a sleep, a swim, a drowning, but even in the dream he battled on. Over the face of the earth the water clamored. Two by two he gathered them, the animals, here at the door of the ark, male and female gathered he them, and here he stood, and *let us in, let us in* they cried, and his robe and his staff he waved, and his white beard he swung to and fro in the blaze of the wind and said to them, saith unto them, *Not by the hair on my chinny-chin-chin.*

And the waters rose, and up over the land and up over the crust of a cloud they elevatored the ark. A pie is what it was, the earth, a giant pie, and the clouds that cobble the earth a patisserie, and he reached out his hand, and partook of what the pie offered, and in his hand he held it -- his hand, his the hand that cuts the pie and fingers the tart and brushes with a knuckle the puff, yea verily, who sucks, from out the belly of the croquemboche, the cream, and licks the cinnamon glaze, and steals the scent of the butter and the almond, and the lemon and the lime, and the ginger and the honey, and the cocoa and the cherry and the dulce de leche. Like unto a god he was.

\* \* \* \* \* \*

Come the dawn Maggie showed. Sat on the bank. Rolled a smoke.

From off the branch that pinned him he plucked a finger of bark. Clawed at the moss in his hair. Called down: "I been meaning to tell you. I got plans for us. Big plans."

"You ain't ripe yet. Maybe tomorrow."

"The hell you say. Look. Lookit. I'm ripe as can be." He touched his forehead. The cheek. Plumpish, like a plum. Lumpish. "Come get me down."

"What do you promise me?"

"The moon."

"I don't got no place to put a moon."

"You got the sky then. I throw in the sky."

"I already got me a sky."

"I swear by the powers – "

"Power don't give a damn what you promise."

"Woman – "

"Shut your mouth." She stood at the base of the tree. The empties pebbled out around her. Up the bank a ways? Butt up in the mud a bottle of Jack. Honey the color. Fat with the ichor of God. Out the waistband of her skirt she fingered up a knob of silk. Tore the fabric. With a twist – like you free a fishhook – she unlimbered the object. Into the fist it went.

"You asked me what it would take. What would it take to win me."

"I got me a plan for -- "

"What was my answer?"

"I got – "

"I wanna hear it. From outta them lips I wanna hear it."

"Nothing. *Nothing* is what you said."

"Nothing. Now look at you. Just look at yourself."

He shut his eyes. Now and again you get, from out the past, an ember to redden the cheek. A singe. Not this. This a furnace. From out the forge in the heart of whoever-the-hell-he-was, a heat.

"But I never – "

"I bought this with my own money." She waited. He stilled himself. Shifted so's to parry the beetle creeping up the cuff of the jean.

"Look," she said.

He looked. She lifted both arms above her head. The right hand a fist, the left hand open, like you see in the movies, the guy on the aircraft carrier who flags the fighter into place for the launch.

"You done won me at last," she said. "You and that nothing of yours."

She opened her fist to reveal, in the palm of the hand, a ring. Fixed him with a look. He followed the ring as, with a twist of the wrist and the fingers, like a magician, she moved to frame it up between the thumb and the finger – an empty O. Over to the other hand now she moved it. Held it in a hover over the tip of the chosen finger.

"Yes or no," she said. "What'll it be?"

He took a breath. From out the blue of the sky a breath, a nothing. Sure the ring a solid thing but the breath, it's the breath that binds. In the crotch of the tree he shifted, made as if to right himself. Slipped. The naked head of a spike, bent by the wind and the wreck of the wind, pierced him. Into the denim and the meat of his thigh hooked, like you gig a fish, the whole of him. It was all he could do to hold it, this breath of his, to give it a shape and a sound of a kind she could answer, she could hear in herself, in the heart of her the torrent as well, the something grand, the something unmendable, the something like a cry.

*Mend* appeared orginally in in Terrain.org (February 2022).

Finalist -- Terrain.org's 12th Annual Fiction Contest

2022 Pushcart Prize Nominee

# Ms. Abbott

by Aaron Morrison

## *It was the height of summer*

when even the evening winds blow warm and don't offer much relief.

We'd distract ourselves from the heat by runnin' and hollerin' like untamed creatures. We'd try and cool off with sips of lemonade our Mas made, and sips of beer offered by our Pas, when our Mas weren't looking of course.

The sun had begun its orangey melt in the sky, when some mix of the heat, too much time on our hands, and just being stupid, shitty kids, led us toward Old Ms.Caroline Abbott's house.

"I heard she murdered a kid."

"Th-th-that's not true, is it?"

"Sure as shit is. Was some stu-stu-stuttering kid, too."

"Th-th-that's not funny."

"My Pa said she's a witch. "

"Bull-shit."

"You calling' my Pa' a liar?"

"I'm sayin' your Pa knows you ain't got nothin' but hog shit for brains, and you believe anything' yer told."

"Shut yer mouth, Porky!"

"Make me, shit-fer-brains!"

Outside her house, the others started tearing up her garden, such as it was, breaking branches off the bushes, throwing mud and rocks at anything their shit aim could hit.

I stood, as if my feet were bound by some entangling vines, and my mind lost in the fog of a dream.

"Run!"

I didn't.

The others were long gone when the front door creaked open, and I had begun to see the edge of Ms. Abbott's silhouette.

I felt the spell break, and I turned and ran home.

~~~

"Yes ma'am... I fully understand... He'll be down tomorrow to make restitution." Pa hung up the phone and turned to me.

"That was Ms. Abbott," Pa said, knowing full well I knew who had called. "You'll be spending the rest of your summer working off your debt."

"The whole summer?"

"Was I not clear, son?"

"But I didn't do anything!"

"And you should think about that."

Pa had a way of speaking in such calm disappointment, that it never failed to make me wish he would just holler, and beat the tar out of me like other kids' fathers did.

The next morning, Pa walked with me over to Ms. Abbott's house, but made me ascend the stairs of her porch alone.

I could hear the echo of the rapping of my knuckles against the thick, but worn, wood of the front door.

The door unlocked and opened so immediately, I imagined she had spent the night standing behind the door waiting for me.

She looked down at me with her cold, blue and gray eyes before looking past me to my Pa. I felt a shiver run up my spine.

"Ma'am."

I knew my Pa had tilted his head all gentlemanly like without looking.

"Here's the boy, as promised. He'll work until you tell him he's done. He knows the way back, so no need to wait on me."

I looked back at my Pa, staggered that he was going to leave me here alone, but I knew better than to argue.

"Thank you, Mr. Ferrell."

Her voice cracked like dried clay in my ears.

Pa nodded once again, and raised an eyebrow at me to let me know more than to mind my manners.

As Pa turned to leave, I looked back at Ms. Abbott, who was staring down at me.

Her white hair was done up in an immaculate bun, matching the tautness of her expression. Her lips pulled tight above the high and choking collar of her dress. Her hand gripped the top of her cane like it would run away if she didn't hold it as such.

"You can start with the front garden."

"Yes ma'am."

She went back inside, shutting the door behind her, and I descended the stairs to begin my duties.

I cleaned up the shattered pots, did what I could to salvage the displaced plants, removed and stacked broken limbs, and pulled weeds from the ground.

I lost track of time, but was becoming aware of the growing pain in my hands.

I heard the front door shut.

I looked up to see a picture of water, a glass, a few plain sandwiches, and a pair of work gloves set on the little table between two chairs.

I eagerly poured and drank a glass of water, and ate a sandwich, as bland as it was.

The gloves were clearly Ms. Abbott's from back when she could do some of this work herself, but I didn't care. They'd at least keep my hands from getting worse.

After several more hours, Ms. Abbott appeared to inspect my work.

"Good enough for today, boy." She tapped her cane on the porch and didn't look at me. "Tomorrow then?"

"Yes, ma'am."

I slept heavily that night, and returned to Ms. Abbott's house right after breakfast.

~~~

A few weeks later, I was busy painting the railings of the porch, when I could hear nattering, like the buzzing of flies on a dog's corpse, approaching.

"Hey shit-fer-brains! We're goin' down to the crick."

"Yeah. Chuck that business and come with."

Without looking, I shook my head, and kept painting.

"Or you rather p-p-play in your l-l-l-lady gloves?"

"Haw haw!"

The flies departed.

I felt the furnace in my ears and face blasting its heat.

"Friends of yours?"

I had no idea how long Ms. Abbott had been standing there.

"No, ma'am." I never felt so sure of something before that point in my life.

"Hm."

Ms. Abbott went back inside and I continued my work in silence.

She returned some time later with a plate of sandwiches and a pitcher of lemonade. "Come on, boy," she said, as she set the items down on the table and sat in one of the two chairs. I ate and drank as we sat in silence.

"Tomorrow then?"

I looked at Ms. Abbott, her hair in a braid over her shoulder, her hands resting in her lap. "Yes, ma'am."

~~~

My work eventually turned to the inside of the house, and my attention was soon pulled to banging, scratching, and sounds of unrest coming from the basement.

I leaned my ear against the door, and slowly began to reach for the handle.

"Boy!" Ms. Abbott called for me from somewhere else in the house.

I left the door alone, though I heard those sounds almost every day I worked there.

Summer came to an end, and I accepted Ms. Abbott's offer to continue my work the following summers, but for pay this time.

It was one of those later days when I picked up a photo album to dust and rearrange a shelf, and a folded picture fell out.

I retrieved the old photograph, and looked at the pretty young woman, who I realized was Ms. Abbott, staring back at me.

Slowly, I began to turn the photograph over, when Ms. Abbott's hand stopped mine. "Sorry. I..."

She gently shook her head.

The noises in the basement grew as loud as I had ever heard them.

"Tomorrow then?"

"Yes, ma'am."

~~~

"I know you've been curious about what's down *there*."

It was the week before I was to move to college.

"Yes ma'am." There was no sense in denying it.

"I suppose I do owe you the truth, but..." she paused for a moment. "Once you learn a thing, there ain't no unlearning it. And this ain't a burden I want to force on your shoulders."

"Whatever it is, I'm choosing' to see."

Ms. Abbott nodded, stood, and led me to the basement door. Her hand shook as she raised the key to the lock.

I lightly placed my hand on her shoulder, and the shaking stopped.

She inserted the key, unlocked, and opened the door.

We descended the stairs together, her right hand on my left arm for balance, and at the bottom I finally saw it.

The source of all the banging, scratching, and sounds of unrest.

The ghosts of her guilt and regret, built up strong from her decades of isolation and self loathing'. A swirling mass of chaos and hurt that,

I imagine, had started as a small, but sturdy seed, and had grown unchecked into the rage that churned around us.

Ms. Abbott looked at me waiting for my condemnation.

I opened my arms to her, and we hugged and wept while the monsters tried, in vain, to reach us.

~~~

Three weeks left in my first semester, my Pa called me to let me know Ms. Abbott had passed on. Her funeral was attended by me, my Ma and Pa, and the pastor.

"Don't let hurt and guilt consume you." Ms. Abbott looked at me with her eyes, gray like the fog of a peaceful morning. "You've seen what it has done to me. And don't let anyone, especially you, snuff out the kindness inside you." Her voice flowed in my ears like a crystal clear brook. "Go and be somethin'."

Dear, Ms. Caroline Abbott.

I think of you often.

I know you are at peace.

And I hope I make you proud.

# BLIND
by Joshua Mahn

## *My Grandpa always told me to avoid that old woodshed*

---

I'd been a good kid most of my life, too. That'd been switched into me young. I was told my daddy got stuck in there real good. Said to "never touch that infernal place." It'd been around since my Granddaddy's daddy was little, maybe more. Said I shouldn't think about it if I knew what was good for me.

I got too big for my britches, I guess.

I remember the scorch marks up along the sides of it where the kerosine burned not-quite-hotter than hell, yet that old punkwood wouldn't yield. I remembered how the circuit riders and itinerant preacher man and even the Wise Ones tried to bless or curse the damn thing but it stood still. Locks never took, they always rusted to bits by suppertime. He tried bricking it up but the mortar never set, not even months after. Said it was an evil place meant to remind us of our sins.

I could hear sounds coming out like coyotes or maybe wildcats fighting in there sometimes. Sometimes it sounded like a man or woman was in there but I was told it was just crows and not to dwell on it and to keep sweet and keep good. I never heard a crow weep like that. I never heard a crow make promises.

No matter now though.

One day my grandaddy and his corn whiskey and his switch scared me more than the stories did and I forgot myself and ran and hid in there. Next thing I knew, the door hid itself from me too. Just old wood everywhere I looked. I could hear him pounding and hollering on the other side, angry and angrier and then sounding scared and then he got all quiet, like he was going further and further away. Or maybe I was. But then there was quiet. And there was the smell of rot and decay and of frankincense and of sulfur. Lanterns hung all about, burning some foul smelling oil, trailing black tendrils of soot, but I was glad I could see a little.

It's not really a woodshed on the inside, you know. It's longer than it is out there.

It's bigger than a church.

Feels more like an attic than a shed, if you can reckon it. I feel like I'm above something else. I'm at the top of whatever this thing is. The way these floorboards creak I know it. I looked down through the cracks and saw what looked like giant wheels turning and spinning and they filled me with a tremendous fear. I tried to remember my prayers but all I could was "Our father, Our father." It all grew terribly loud, sounding like water rushing all over my head, like I was drowning. "Our father, Our father." Nothing else came.

I closed my eyes and got up and the noise stopped.

I ran on and on, hoping to make some sense of it all but all I could see was empty sigogglin barn stalls with dried up husks inside. Skeletons with their skin stretched leathery thin, pigs and cows and horses and dogs and my daddy in his Sunday best who looked to have died with a scroll stuck in his mouth.

I couldn't even weep.

I walked on, past more stalls and more. Past a skeleton tied up with rope and laying on its side which spoke to me in a crow's voice, "You shall surely die."

Past piles of smoldering shit with bread baking atop. Past a scale laden with hair and two further piles next to it, measured for some alien purpose. Skeletons of all sizes with human teeth marks all over, some seeming to gnaw on each other even yet.

As I walked, I could see something writ in dark soot on the floor, it read;

"Now is the end come upon thee, and I will send mine anger upon thee, and will judge thee according to thy ways, and will recompense upon thee all thine abominations.

Mine eye shall not spare thee, neither will I have pity. I will recompense thy own ways upon thee, and thine abominations shall be in the midst of thee, and ye shall know what I am.

Thus saith I; An evil, an only evil, behold, is come."

The lettering grew smeared and worn for some time, yet it did grow legible once more.

"Go ye through the city, and smite. Let not your eye spare, neither have ye pity;

Slay utterly old and young, both maids and children and women.

Defile the house, and fill the courts with the slain. Go ye forth."

I trembled and I walked on and finally I wept.

At last I saw a large room. A sanctuary, and at its front was a pulpit made of precious stones all twinkling like beetles in this dim light. My name was written in crimson upon its face.

Atop it was a scroll, and on both sides of it were written words of lamentation and mourning and joy. Such joy! It tasted of honey and I swallowed it whole without choking. "Look for the mark upon the forehead," it taught me. "And begin with the aged in front of the temple."

Just beyond it a door.

Grandaddy doesn't scare me much anymore.
I'm bigger than church.

# LUCK

by Nicholas Michael Reeves

as it goes -- belongs in
bad novels, and is most often
found in the anatomy

of strangers closing down
dark bars on the outskirts
of town. It's often an aside
of the jealous, a half-hearted

insult, or a lie born of
lightbulbs in Vegas.

But luck, to me,
is the conversation I had
with the angel whose home
is the tip of this pen.

Luck is watching the little ships
setting sail in the puddle, off to
their very own Neverland.

Luck is the nation of ants
invading France in the form of a
half-eaten, day-old macaroon.

There is no copper
Abe lying heads up
on a sidewalk

and no tiled
fountain so lucky
as this.

This lucky day,
the sun doing everything
it can to strike you

as if you were the
last match in his box.

# SIXTY-WATT

*by Nicholas Michael Reeves*

What's that? The boy asked.

It's an old fable called stars, his grandfather told him. Some say there were sheep and gods and arrows and strings in the sky. The whole night was theatre, your window the silver screen. You could look in the telescope and see the little old man on his rickety ladder, screwing in sixty-watt bulbs against the dark—because no more fish were biting, and his ass hurt, from sitting on the moon.

What happened to him?

Nothing, he told the boy. He's still up there, tinkering. We've just made too much light here on earth.

# THE TRUNK

BY AARON MORRISON

*The frigid, icy air sweeping across his face wakes the boy*

As the fog drifts from his eyes, he begins to see white gliding beneath him, and, on the outskirts of his vision, a wall of snow-dusted pine trees.

Then he becomes aware of the pain.

An uncaring hand hauls the boy over the ground by his neck, pulling at his skin and hair. The boy begins to thrash and scream.

The man makes no effort to quiet him.

The only response the boy receives to his cries are the crunching of snow beneath the man's boots, and the echo of his own screams bouncing off the ever neutral conifers.

The boy continues to struggle as the man ascends the three wooden steps to the porch of the cabin and, with his free hand, opens the unlocked door.

The man's heavy, unbroken stride brings them both to the seward trunk looming at the far end of the room.

The lid is swung open. The boy is thrown inside.

The lid slams down, and darkness now surrounds him.

The clacking of latches and then nothing but the smell of pine and piss to accompany the darkness.

The boy screams and kicks and cries out for his mother until he lacks the energy to continue. He quivers as his cries give way to gasping sobs, and his face is soaked in tears and snot and spit. The boy begins to feel a deep exhaustion and uncontrollable sleep.

For a moment, he feels arms, similar to his own, around him, and he cries no more.

—

The noises from the trunk die down, and with it, the voice should be quiet.

For a few days at least.

Seated in the single chair at the small, circular table in the kitchen, the man peels back the cellophane on his meal with his left hand, and watches the steam rise and dissipate in the cold air like a specter.

Left hand rests back on the table, as the right hand reaches and pulls the tab on a silver can of beer. Three gulps of the liquid and the can is placed back in the exact spot from which it came.

He lifts his fork, and presses the edge through the minced meat of the Salisbury steak. He pierces the soft chunk, slides it through the gravy, raises it to his mouth, and places it inside.

Chewing slowly and silently, he lowers the fork, and rests his hand on the table. A forkful of corn.

A forkful of too creamy mashed potatoes that taste better when dragged through gravy. A sip of beer.

Repeat until the meal is complete,

He replaces the cellophane over the accusing eyes and shouting, frowning mouth of the container.

He takes the final sip of beer, stands, places the can and container in the trash can, and carefully washes the fork.

After placing the fork on the folded towel next to the sink, he washes and dries his hands, and turns off the water.

His heavy steps take him to his bedroom, where he sits on the edge of the bed, and removes his boots.

Still fully clothed, he turns and lies down on the bed.

Hands folded across his chest, he waits, open eyed, for time to pass.

Sleep will come if it wants.

—

*Filthy fucker. Like your father.*

*Left us.*

*Left me.*

*Left to fuck Linda from the diner.*

*You look just like him.*

*You look just like that filthy fuck.*

*Get in the trunk.*

*GET THE TRUNK!*

She slaps and strikes him and shoves him inside.

He wets the bed, and tries to hide his soiled sheets, but of course she finds him. She shoves them in his face before locking him in the trunk for an hour.

He puts another forkful of food in his mouth before fully finishing the previous one. He clinks his fork too loudly when setting down.

She shoves handfuls of the food into his face.

*Filthy fucking pig! Disgusting fucking animal!*

Into the trunk for half an hour.

He's caught touching himself.

She strikes his hand and offensive member with the thin, wooden rod that she had removed from the laundry rack some time ago. He's too big for the trunk, but the closet she put the heavy door and bolts on will do. *Filthy!*

*Filthy!*

*Filthy!*

*Filthy!*

*Filthy!*

"Filthy."

He stands naked in the bathroom and stares at himself in the mirror.

The wooden rod from the laundry rack gripped tightly in his shaking right hand. He strikes his left hand. His chest. His genitals.

He vomits in the shower.

—

Ice creaks beneath his boots as he carries an ice saw, and the empty husk of the last boy he put in the trunk, out toward the center of the lake.

The slightly warmer than usual winter makes the ice easier to cut, and soon enough he has a hole just large enough to drop the body down.

The rocks he added to the boy's pockets help drag his body down into the frigid waters to join the others at the bottom.

The man returns to his cabin as nature already begins to seal the hole behind him.

—

The detective sits at his desk and looks around to see if anyone is looking at him.

Third shift never pays him any mind when he stays late, but still, he doesn't want to make it obvious.

He pours whiskey from the flask into his coffee, and quickly hides the thing away again.
*An alcoholic fuck. Just like my dad.*

He should probably just go home, but what was he going to do there? Get drunk and look at filthy magazines most likely.

At least here, he could get drunk and still work on the case.

*I guess I became a detective to try and help people, and prove I was better than my dad. But two failed marriages later, I guess I'm more like him than I'd like to admit.*

It was the most honest thing he had shared in his mandatory meetings with the psychologist.

Everything else was just saying what he needed to say to get through his two week suspension, with pay.

He heard screaming and shouting coming from a neighbor's house, and he walked down to investigate the disturbance.

He had seen the tell tale signs of abuse before, but it had all been aftermath.

This time, he sees her freshly busted lip and her broken, bleeding nose as her husband openly raises his fist in their front yard.

His gun made sure he'd never hurt her again.

*I saw my dad's face on that fucker.*

He doesn't share that part.

His suspension has been up for a week, and he's been back on the serial kidnapping case. *We will do everything we can. We have our best men on it.*
He tells the truth to the parents of the missing boys, as empty as it is.

He leaves out the statistics of time passed to likelihood of finding a missing person.

He leaves out that their best man is an alcoholic who skips sleep too often, and when he does sleep, it's usually in the office rather than in his own bed.
A stack of cases over the years, and not one goddamn lead.

One missing kid after another. No bodies. No notes. No ransom demands. Just someone preying on the innocent.

Years ago, his second wife asked him why he never went to church with her. *Not sure I believe in anything anymore. Other than in the filth that is humanity.* He didn't blame Brenda for leaving him three days later.

—

The man sits in his car, watches and waits.

He needs to silence the voice again.

*That one. He looks like a bed wetter. He looks like you. He looks like your filthy, fucking father. He needs to be punished.*

He sees no one else around, so he does what he's always done before.

Pop the trunk.
Car still running.
No convincing or trickery.
Long strides from behind.
Hand over mouth.
Quick injection.
Limp and light body tossed in the trunk.
Back to the cabin.
Voice will be quiet for a few days at least.

—

Another boy was taken.

But finally a break.

A witness.

A convenient spy who saw some of what happened.

The detective enters the room as calmly as he can, and quickly introduces himself to the mother and child.

"Can you tell me what you saw?"

The child looks to their mother for reassurance.

"It's okay, honey. Tell the nice detective what you saw."

"A man took Billy. Put him in his car and drove away."

"Did you see the man's face?"

A shake of the head.

"What kind of... can you draw the car?" The detective pushes a notepad and pen at the kid. The kid nods and begins to draw. "What color was it?"

"Yellow."

"Draw any numbers or letters you saw on the back of the car.

The kid writes a "B" and a "9".

"How did the car sound?"

"Kind of loud. Like a growl and it was clicking."

"Anything else you remember?"

A shake of the head.

"You did great." The detective takes the picture and, as soon as he is out of the room, runs to the officer manning the computer teletype.

"Get this search to the DMV now," the detective orders.

"It's only two..."

"I fucking know. It's a yellow Chrysler Cordoba, so narrow it down."

The officer looks incredulously at the kid's drawing, but starts the search. "Find me as soon as you have something."

—

Police cars race as fast as they dare go on the slushy roads.

The detective's car fishtailed a few times, giving a warning to the following vehicles. They have a name and an address.

They race past the private property signs and through the pines.

The detective stops as soon as he sees the yellow Chrysler Cordoba outside the cabin.

He leads the officers, hunched and running, to the cabin, and signals for one to start circling toward the back.

His shaking, but determined, hand reaches for the door which, unlocked, opens with ease. A trunk sits in the far corner of the room.

A man standing in the kitchen looks at the detective, hesitates for a moment, then turns and runs.

The detective chases after him, and is too far away to hear the cry of pure anguish from the officer who opens the trunk.

—

The man turns to see police entering his cabin and, after a moment of hesitation, turns to run out the back.

He bursts through the back door, stumbles briefly, then continues his sprint as he ignores the shouts of "stop!" and "freeze!" and "we'll shoot you, you bastard!"

His boots hit the ice of the lake hard, and a sound like the rubbing of styrofoam ripples out from beneath his feet.

As he reaches the middle of the lake, he turns to see the two policemen, guns drawn, slip to a halt as the one wearing a tie reaches a hand out to stop the one wearing a uniform.

The man turns all the way around to fully look at them, and takes a step backward. He stumbles as the ice cracks beneath him and gives way.

As he falls, he reaches out and grabs the front of the dress of his mother, still spewing her vitriol. Dozens of small hands grab onto the man, and pull him down into the freezing abyss.

—

# THE FANTODS
## BY GABRIEL MCLEOD

### *It happened again last night*

Somewhere between drifting off and full REM, in some ether-middle-realm of dream and awake, sleep paralysis seizes me. It begins as an ice-cold wave wash over me, covers or not. The cold starts with my spine and all my hairs stand on end. I can open my eyes and see the shadow outlines of my bed and room but I cannot move at all. In my peripheral vision I can see a shadowy twitching presence. Can feel a being behind me, slowly moving atop of me either on my chest or neck. Can feel an icy breath on my scalp. I scream within my mind but no sound comes out. If I give into the dream realm, I feel myself being lifted, levitating beyond my control. If I stay half awake, I fight it mentally but motionless. It lasts minutes but feels like hours. I find my way back but usually never sleep again the rest of the night.

These used to only be once or twice a year but lately I can expect these strange visitations more often. My therapist once told me it was residuals of stress caused by my latent depression and anxiety. It also echoes a post traumatic stress disorder. But I am not so sure. Sometimes I worry it is something much darker coming for me. My family has always had a proclivity to paranormal encounters.

Grandma suffered from the fantods quite often. To counteract those ill feelings, she used a variety of self-medications, rituals, ceremonies mixed with a plethora of tokens, charms, amulets and coins all held together in her gris-gris bag. You could hear her magic jingle as she walked.

Fantods were more than feeling, they were supernatural. She felt vibrations and sensations that none of us did and used it as a guiding force. We could walk into a room or a restaurant and if she felt a bad vibe, she would sniff the four directions and if her own personal magic couldn't quelch or calm the feeling that she felt she would exclaim, "Ooh lord, my fantods. Uh-uh my Honeychiles, we gots to go."

She had a power that came from a strength of prayer not only to God but to all the magical creatures and nature spirits everywhere and held the uncanny ability to turn any bad thing into a positive outcome. She could cure sicknesses and mend broken hearts.

When my cousin went missing and those prayers and power couldn't bring her back, I knew there were dark forces out there that were greater than all of us. My cousin going missing began the downfall of my Grandma and when she began to doubt herself. Doubting herself began the opening of a door for all sorts of dark things that came to our family. I know it was all my fault.

My family has always lived close to swamps, bayous and backwaters, going back for generations. Partly it was the water but I think it was also the calling towards the dark, damp earth. There is something ancient about that topography. We were a mixture of Accadian, Alabamu, Chitimacha, Creole, Irish and Scottish. It seems the matriarchs and patriarchs of my genealogy often met from different backgrounds but something in their spirits drew them back towards this primordial landscape. Our people were drawn to where the water met the land and created a different type of place. Young'uns wore mud more than socks.

My folks worked a lot and when they weren't working, they drank and fought and I was always just in the way. They sent me off to live with my Grandparents during Summers and holidays and eventually I just lived there all the time. We had a lot of relatives and cousins around, some that weren't even blood.

One Sunday there was a Fais Dodo planned and everyone woke up early cooking. Varieties of fine aromas filled the street, wafting in from the houses on the block.

My cousin, Lilith, and I played in the dark on the outskirts of the swamp all afternoon. Uncle Zeke called her Lilith Luck because she had this natural luck streak in her bones. She could always find a four-leaf clover in any field, always find a blue jay feather and always pick the good numbers on the scratch offs family and friends would bring by.

A hog was slowly turning over the fire and pots full of beans simmered. Adults played boo-ray and domino while the teenagers played catch. Old folks played the fiddle and some danced in the street.

We were in that "little stage" – too old to be babies, too young to be even close to teenagers... just little kids more interested in exploring and playing our own games than joining the others.

We had filled up on pickled quail eggs and hot water corn cakes earlier so we weren't hungry and the darkening hour had begun where you could see lightning bugs appear in the backyard. Behind all of our backyards was the swamp.

Some called it Ol' Black Swamp, some called it Sinful Swamp, others called it other things. But it was a comforting source of stories, fear and food for all of us.

The swamp stretched for miles and miles and held stories of Rougarou and Boo Hags, not to mention all the snakes and gators and other critters. There was even a story of a college professor that fell in love with a Banshee in those swamps and lived to write a book about it. We were always warned never to go in there. Which, I guess, is why I was so tempted.

We went catching lightning bugs under the edge of trees that circled Ol' Black Swamp. Dragonflies, or Hirondelles as Grandma would say, darted in and out. Looking back now, I reckon they were warning us to stay away.

Among the darting lightning bugs hoovered a larger light that began to circle above it, dropping down in front of Lilith's face. It would come right up to the tip of her nose, causing her whole face to glow in the dusk and then back away, causing her to follow. I had heard stories about the Fifolet before, but we just thought this was the biggest firefly we had ever seen. It would come up, dip down, pull back as if it wanted her to follow deeper under the trees, deeper into the swamp. She stopped and grew scared. She was younger and smaller than me and I was in charge of her protection when we played. But I dared her to follow the light and not be such a baby.

As we entered the swamp, we couldn't hear the laughter or the music from the party in the street, only the sounds of the dark.

The light darted, hovered, caressed and cajoled her to keep following. We didn't notice the shallow water as we walked, her following the teasing light, me close behind. The light found its way against the trunk of a giant Cypress tree. It went around the backside but then darted to her and, I swear, beckoned her forward. It went into a hollow opening of the tree. It hung there in the space, like the last ornament on a Christmas tree. Little freesons, goosebumps some say, spread all over my arms. She stepped into that hollow and reached out to put her tiny hand on the light. She curled her fingers around it and looked at me to say something but then the light went out and all went dark. All was dark save for the moon through the Spanish moss covered branches. I stepped into the opening of the tree and she was not there. Nothing but shadow. Somewhere a bullfrog laughed.

I called her name and felt around the hollow. I ran around the tree and screamed... she was gone.

I ran back to the street party, crying mad and scared. The men went running into Black Swamp immediately with flashlights. It was all a blur, the grownups, the teenagers, everyone hollering and amidst it all was my Grandma staring at me with her eyes pooling with tears, shaking her head.

She went into the house and gathered all her Hoodoo items she could carry, putting on her big black frog gigging boots on. Paw Paw wasn't there, he was a Vagabond and Raconteur and drifted for weeks at a time. Grandma was the force that held us all, family and friend and foe alike, together.

She marched into the swamp with a confidence that felt like God was riding piggybacked on her shoulders. I trailed behind her scared. Scared of being in trouble, scared for Lilith, scared of all the commotion and chaos and scared of life itself.

Grandma had been going in and out of that swamp since she was my age and treated it like an extension of her own property. But on this day, as soon as she hit the tree line at the swamp mouth she froze in place. She looked at me with fear in her face and said "Oh lord, the fantods. I feel them all over. This ain't good, ain't good at all."

I took her to the tree where I last saw Lilith and watched as the eyes rolled up in the back of her head and she swayed in place. I looked up at the constellations, far away through the blanket of tree tops. Up in a tree beside us was the shape of a bobcat staring down with human eyes instead of feline. Men and women crawled crazy through the mud and water and trees like ants on a spilled picnic and in the middle of it all, Grandma began to sing.

It was a low and soft song, an old song in an ancient language. I don't know if it was French or Gaelic or something else but it was words that seemed familiar but also sad. As she sang the swamp grew quiet, the people grew still. They began to circle back to where she stood and sang, her song growing louder and my family and their friends began to sing along.

Nothing was ever the same after that day. That day, I could feel them grow up through my heels like cold roots, the fantods began to bloom inside of me too.

That was many, many moons ago but the feeling is as fresh now as it was then. That was the fall of my family, we never recovered. I moved away in time, out to the city. Tried to reinvent myself many times, in many towns. But everywhere I go, the ghosts follow me. I see things others do not see, feel things others do not feel. I carry the swamp on my shoulders.

My therapist gave me a list of all the reasons why sleep paralysis overtakes me, but I now know better. There is something coming for me. I have denied that side for too long. Instead of running from the darkness, I need to turn and embrace it.

Within that darkness, I will find a light. Be it a Fifolet or Firefly, I will find it and follow it fearlessly.

# The Angel and Elvis
## by Darryl Pickett

### *Dedicated to the memory of Suzanna Leigh*

---

### Winter Garden, Florida

In November of 2010, I moved out of my apartment in one of the most tourist-choked ends of Highyway 192, at the west end of Kissimmee, deep in the heart of theme park central. Two nights prior, I had attended a production of *Noises Off* at the Garden Theatre. I also had dinner at Thai Blossom, a restaurant that one of my fellow actors had opened within the Edgewater Hotel. "Why the hell don't I live here?" I asked myself.

A week later, I had broken my previous lease in Kissimmee and rented an apartment not far from Winter Garden's fast-growing downtown. It was a life-changing decision, made impulsively on the basis of a good meal and watching friends perform in a classic farce. Now I could escape the clamor and sensory overwhelm of the theme parks, and center myself in a small town ambiance far from Disney.

Winter Garden afforded me access to excellent food, a nascent arts scene, and perhaps best of all, a sprawling network of bike trails that would allow me to keep exercising my way to health and fitness.

I didn't really begin to know myself until I made this move. I told people at the time that the rural atmosphere agreed with me. ("I have a big city heart but a rural nervous system," I often told friends.) I fell in love with the community, conservative as it was, though I was fast evolving into an advocate of social justice, newly aware of the inequities from which I had long benefited. Externally, I wore the mask of agreeability and normality. I didn't know that someone was about to come into my life who would help me to face who I really was with honesty and courage.

My coworker and friend Tracey lived nearby. That July, she invited me to her birthday party. It was there that I met Suzanna Leigh.

I was already an ardent fan of Hammer horror, so I had seen Suzanna in *The Lost Continent, Lust For a Vampire,* and *The Deadly Bees.* I owned these films and rewatched them pretty frequently. Tracey led me to her. I wasn't expecting to meet anyone famous. I didn't recognize her right away.

"This is Suzanna," said Tracey. "She's our local celebrity. She was in a movie with Elvis." I knew instantly knew who she was, whose hand I was now shaking.

I'll never forget her first words to me. "Hello, darling. Forgive me, but I've had a few drinks, so I'm feeling a bit randy!"

Was one of my early screen crushes flirting with me? It was such a surreal moment. I remember calling my brother in New Mexico that same night and telling him about it. I didn't know that she would become my friend, or how much she would mean to my new life in Winter Garden. I was simply delighted at the unexpected surprise of it.

My first novel, *The Secret Feast of Father Christmas,* was published in 2010. A year later, I took part in a local Christmas event, booking a table in front of a used book store on Plant Street, ready to sign and sell copies of my book. To my astonished surprise, Suzanna had a table right next to mine. She was doing the same thing with copies of her autobiography, *Paradise Suzanna Style.* We were both asked questions about our books. I overheard Suzanna summarizing her life story while I had the task of making my coming-of-age story set in New Zealand sound as interesting. I'm sure she signed and sold more books than I did, but anytime the crowds subsided, she talked to me, wanting to know more about who I was, my Disney career, and what had brought me to Winter Garden.

"If I sign a copy and give it to you, will you sign a copy of yours and give it to me," she asked.

I answered "Of course I would," and that exchange of literary debuts cemented our friendship. My signed copy of *Paradise Suzanna Style* is one of my most treasured possessions, even after downsizing and minimizing my physical belongings several times since.

Suzanna would find me several times a week at Axum Coffee, a local cafe that provides charitable donations to local and global causes, emphasizing sustainable food and water systems for disadvantaged communities. During my ten year residency in Winter Garden, Axum was my writer's roost. (A healthy chunk of the book you now hold in your hands was written there.) Suzanna saw me as a fellow writer. She would often sit at the table with me, always making sure to ask if I minded. We sat side by side, always with good intentions of getting work done, but as often as not, she ended up regaling me with stories, which I listened to eagerly.

Her most iconic star moment was a publicity photo of her kissing Elvis Presley. She and the King had been strictly platonic on the set of *Paradise, Hawaiian Style*, though Suzanna was candid about the strong physical attraction they had for one another. In her book, she describes the moments when their lips met.

*"His kisses held an intensity that melted my very being. I slipped my arms around his neck and our bodies entwined. This was all madness but we didn't stop. A person could go to the gallows with such a kiss lingering on their lips and know that life had been good."**

Heck, after reading that, I wanted to kiss Elvis too! She had a gift for letting the reader feel as if they had lived her experiences themselves.

I was no longer a staff writer at Disney. I was trying to make my way as an independent consultant, while also working as an actor and a part time cast member at the parks. At one point, I was holding down four jobs at once and still struggling to make ends meet.

Suzanna would invite me to her small bungalow home and make me a nutritious lunch. At other times, she brought me fresh baked goods or a Thermos full of soup to take home with me. She would call to me across Plant Street when she was dining with friends at the Chef's Table so I could join them. She treated me as a friend, an equal, a fellow traveler. She was so kind. I never felt I had done anything to earn this. I wasn't alone. She extended this kindness to everyone.

Suzanna often attended fan conventions and shows, selling autographed pictures and copies of her book. (She once asked me if I knew how to add watermarks to files to prevent their unauthorized duplication. I was happy to help.) She once sat next to the great Christopher Lee at a signing table. "Ah, I see you brought the legs," Lee remarked. She replayed the moment for me, doing a great impersonation of Lee, complete with ironically disapproving mien and honeyed vocal tone.

She had no airs about her. She treated her fellow Winter Gardenians with the same respect and empathy she showed to cinema royalty. By proxy, we felt connected to legends. We mattered just as much as they did.

Around this time, I was diagnosed with both Generalized Anxiety Disorder and Type II Diabetes. In order to remain healthy, productive and just plain functional, I tried to ride my bike every morning. I was determined keep my weight in check. Looking back through photographs, I can easily trace my yo-yo pattern of rapid weight loss and quick backsliding. My ever-languishing finances made it a challenge to buy clothes to match my now-svelte now-plump physique. Deep down, I knew I would need the baggy clothes again. I lived in a constant state of self-consciousness and imposter syndrome. Suzanna saw me as she knew I could be, instead of the way I too often saw myself.

One afternoon, after I had shed a lot of weight through medication and a change of diet, she spotted me behind the Garden Theatre. I was wearing a large orange shirt that billowed around me like a tent. She wasn't having it. "Oh no! That will never do! I want to see you in something tight and clinging, you sexy man!"

No one could have made me feel better in that moment than she did. The memory still helps me when I need to believe in myself but my mind is reluctant to allow it.

In 2017, Suzanna was diagnosed with Stage 4 liver cancer. She let me know about it one afternoon as we shared some nutritious snacks at the Plant Street Market. She was optimistic about the diagnosis, counting on a regimen of fruits, vegetables, and supplements to turn the tide. I believed in her, in spite of my concern and my skepticism. She couldn't possibly lose this battle with that attitude, that strength.

But I saw her less and less often. When I did, I could see that the fight was taking its toll. She still summoned her most positive attitude and never stopped looking forward. She was even writing, and talking about her next book.

The last time I ever saw her was at the local ALDI store, just weeks before she passed. She was with her daughter Natalia. She introduced me, though I had met Natalia at least twice before. I could see at a glance that Suzanna was suffering, that Natalia was valiantly taking on the burden of caring for her. I knew there was nothing to be gained from me trying to reach out to Suzanna or talk to her anymore. The end was now inevitable. When I got home, I cried.

Suzanna Leigh died on December 11, 2017. I was already grieving the loss when I read the obituary. I've never stopped thinking about my good fortune in having made such a friend. I was so lucky to have known her.

I returned to my native New Mexico at the end of 2020, when the pandemic brought the entire themed entertainment industry to a stop. Natalia Leigh has dedicated herself to preserving her mother's legacy. She graciously sent me one of my favorite photographs of Suzanna, a photo taken at the London premiere of the movie *Born Free* in which Suzanna met Queen Elizabeth, along with Raquel Welch, James Fox, and Woody Allen. It's a portrait of a truly unique moment in time. It hangs on my wall to remind me of the unexpected connections that link every one of us. If I'm six degrees of separation from Kevin Bacon, Suzanna tells me that I'm no more than two degrees separated from Elvis, Christopher Lee, Peter Cushing, Ringo Starr, Harry Nillson, countless others. And I'm never more than one degree from Suzanna herself.

I love you. Rest in eternal power, Suzanna Leigh.

*This passage is taken from Paradise Suzanna Style, copyright © Suzanna Leigh 2000, ISBN 1-4392-0968-5*

# I DONE HAVE
by Nicholas Michael Reeves

## *I sit by your grave and pick the dead damp grass*

It's done raining and there's a little moon in every leaf.

I'm dog tired mama, but I can't sleep. Gun on my nightstand wants too much to do with me.

You used to say lies can't never go to sleep, mother. Member that?

I wonder what's keeping you up down there, eyes wide open, lying in your Sunday best, hands clenched in prayer. I reckon I'll know sooner. Every casket this family closes lets out another secret.

Last you wrote to me, some months ago: *One of these days we can catch up and you can talk into my casket.* So I got drunk before I came here. You scare me even when you're dead.

I was membrin' the way you used to drag me here every Sunday after church, talking to all them wooden overcoats. Tryin to put a lifetime into words to the only folks who ever understood you without them. But you can't lie to mothers. You know I ain't fine and I don't miss you not who you become anyways and I know you can hear me cos lies don't sleep.

I remember I'd ask you why the graves crack?

The dead crackin 'up at our lies, you'd say.

You joked we kept the florist in business. All those Sundays are hotter'n hell. I sweated through that tweed suit you knitted me, like some flower boy for the dead.

Now I'm a decade older wishin I hadn't come home from war. Ain't slept a wink since. The gun on my nightstand wants too much to do with me.

You awake down there mama? Lies don't sleep.

Like all those hungry nights, do you remember? Not a licka sleep. We were poor as the dirt we lived on, Mama. Weren't we? Prayed all winter. Spring, silent spring. Sterile summer, Mother. Just like you, 'fore me. Year after year, like that. So you brought in the borders, peg-legged, glass-eyed men with suspicious suitcases.

"Daddy'll send money, son. I just know he will."

The crows cowed and cursed; no one ever saw such skinny crows.

You read me bedtime stories so I wouldn't go to bed so hungry. That hunger is precious to me. Even still. I want to be hungry like that again. Like those crows.

Do you remember when the crows ate the scarecrow?

You said daddy's keeping us safe.

But I watched the crows eat daddy. Back when I called him daddy, 'fore I knew he was dead dead and not ever coming home. Daddy in his old red flannel and Levi's. Copenhagen ring. Cigarette burns. We resurrected him with some garden twine. Broomstick spine. A hammer and nails. Like Jesus. Old Jesus.

In the blood meridian the old tin colander hat drooled gold. Looked like the crows drank the rust. That little boy didn't know he'd go to war one day and find his father in every dead soldier, lying strewn like scarecrows, like daddy, under rusted helmets, young bones jut out like broomsticks.

"Father can scare anything off," you had said, your hand on your stomach.

I began to understand the miscarriages. You are carrying the weight of what you once carried. How the dead weight of nothing is heavier than the weight of nothing.

I was too young to be that old, mama.

But you dragged me to the family plot again and again. All my dead sisters and brothers. They made me, I swear it so. Seven months pregnant with Lucy, you told father, "I feel empty. It's the heaviest thing." How on earth, I wondered, is emptiness the heaviest feeling?

I remember thinking the veins in your legs looked like roots in a dying tree.

"Does daddy believe in God?"

"He's dead," you said.

"Does God believe in daddy?"

You didn't answer.

110

"How Bout when he wasn't dead?"

"Daddy didn't need God. A drinkin' man's his own god."

"Is daddy really dead?" I asked you.

You wept. I knew then, the dead live in our hearts.

I found an old liquor bottle under the floorboard. It smelled like how I remembered him. I drank til I threw up. Your father drank himself into an elegy I'll never finish writing, you said. And here you are, becoming him.

One night you burned all the photographs.

Go to hell, you whispered to him. Hell, you sent him there. The charred, crozzled edges, proof. All I could see was father's head cut off from his blue-jeaned overalled torso. The hand of his ghost on my shoulder.

God quit with the rain. We choked on our supper. Dust, our daily bread. I learned there ain't nothin more expensive than being poor.

Your skin paled the color of the lone white rose you pressed into the family Bible. Time ate your bones. You rang the neck of every last chicken. They rang like broken bells. I covered my ears when I heard them dying. We sucked dry the bones.

You stole from the offering plate and that's why Brother Charlie kicked us out of Black Creek Baptist.

One evening I came back from the barn wearing Daddy's boots. They were so big I couldn't walk, I kept falling out of them. But two years passed and the pencil marks on the pantry wall started to fly. I tried the shoes on every month, religiously, feeling my feet in his.

You stopped calling me Clifton, because it reminded you of daddy.

I hated being the second. Clifton Henry Ross II.

Once, I opened my eyes mid-prayer. Your eyes bore a hole through me. It was winter. The soup was cold.

I read Frankenstein three times in a row. The monster, my only friend. Where the hell is father? I asked you.

You said don't talk about him no more, son.

I really am a son of a bitch, I told you.

You said you want to see your father go look in the mirror.

Mirra. That goddamn southern tongue.

You were an open wound: when you spoke, you bled. I was your

Passover. I never met any angels.

No wonder father left, I told you.

You said it sure as hell don't take a big person to carry a grudge.

Livin proof you are, I spat back.

You quit speaking to me. You played piano like an altar. Til arthritis ate your fingers and I found the lid of the piano locked.

I quit going to church.

You said Gods gonna take your name out of his book. I said I don't care for what Bible you're reading. Where you saw a sinner, I saw a story. Where you saw darkness, I saw light. If this is God I'll go to hell.

You were angry, so you needed God to be. You gave Jesus everything but your heart. That's all I had to give him.

Then I won the lottery. Reading the draft notice, I remembered what granddaddy had said: Killin' people ain't good for ya, son.

It sure ain't, mama. I did kill so many.

Mother, I wrote to you. Tell me the truth about father 'fore I become him.

You said Son, you have done it.

I sit by your grave and pick the dead damp grass. I have done it.

It's done raining and there's a little moon in every leaf and I have.

Gun on my nightstand wants too much to do with me, Mama.

I lie on your stone. Close my eyes. I have done it.

# SUGAR

## BY ALAN SINCIC

"... Sal. But Sal – that building's got nothing in it, and you don't got any customers – what the hell you need a guard dog for?"

Sal explains it to me. If you ever want to get bigger – even have a chance of getting bigger – you got to pretend to be bigger than you actually are. It's not *Two Guys Gluing Together Roof Windows in an Empty Room*. That's not the name of the company. It's not *Don and Billy's Roof Windows* or even *Don and Billy's Skylights* or even *Sunny Sun-Shiney Skylights* or even *Sun-Tek Skylights*, no. It's *Sun-Tek Industries*. It's an industry, see. You gotta be the butterfly with the spot on the wing that looks like the eye of the giant screech-owl. Scare off the predators. That's the idea behind the guard at the gate, see, but guard dogs one and two are a narcoleptic Doberman puppy and an Irish Setter with ADD, Dyslexia, Tourette's Syndrome and an inexplicable fear of pancakes. So that'd make Sugar -- see? -- Sugar the go-to dog.

"Sugar... Sugar...." Sal backpedals up the drive, the hose tucked under her armpit as she shouts, claps her hands to her thighs, jiggles the hips to make herself a more appetizing prey.

I'm already en route to my morning nap, three beers into breakfast, two ticks shy of horizontal on my reclino-matic lawn-chair. "You got to get closer, Sal. Try the other ear."

"Sugar!"

Say you were going to build a dog. Say you had a dog factory, end of the week you had a bunch of left-over doggy parts laying around, you bang together your own little home-made dog, home-style, amateur dog, not a professional dog with GPS and cruise control and a plush leather seat, but a dog that don't got no papers -- not even to poop on: a Kmart collapsible no-deposit no-return polyester-furred port-a-dog just big enough to fit in the overhead compartment. That'd be the kind of dog I'm talking about when I talk about this dog, this dog Sugar. My sister named her – scooped her up off the street, she was a hobo dog – named her *Sugar* for the finger-licking sweetness of her disposition. Big mistake. Big mistake. Sweet and sour's more like it. Smells like mold, sheds like a chunk of burnt toast but, it's all of it, it's a calculation, see? That ani-mule, that grifter, that Tinker-Toy tower of animated table-scraps. Dog deserves an Academy Award if you ask me, that limp of hers, no not on one leg, no, that'd be too easy, but all over at the same time, like a shopping cart with a snagged wheel. *Wobble-wobble-hiccup, wobble-wobble-hiccup.* And oh poor baby she don't bark, the bark got broken back there somehow, so she *raspitt... raspitt... raspitt...* coughs instead. That's her happy cough. *Chuff-chuff-chuff...* that's her excited cough. *Hwope-hwope-hwope...* that's her mournful cough.

Don't you be fooled by that. Do not let her seduce you. Do not let her look you in the eye with that one good eye of hers, do not let her force you to –

Love is a torment. Love is a torture. Take this girl I been seeing – Angie. Not dating, no, she's married but, you know... seeing. Gets on the phone, see? Cooking up this rendezvous. Strange what a big deal you can make outta just a spoonful of air. *I love you* she says. I breath it right back at her, that same exhalation of nothingness. "I love you too." Goddam ridiculous, I know, but what can you say? Every which way you turn you got somebody chipping, chipping away, wanting a piece out of you.

And now this. So-called Sugar? *Hwope-hwope-hwope.* Christ on a cracker. Second she comes bubbling up out of the compost I can see it, I can see it coming. *Hwope-hwope. Sugar The Wonderdog* I call her for her skill, tick-tick-tick of the tail, at orchestrating every damn event to her advantage. Even her ears sticking out every which way – mark my words – they're some kind of finely-tuned piece of secret machinery: one ear up, one ear down, like tinfoil flags on a TV antenna teetering, in a blizzard of static, to freeze on that one clear channel home.

"Sal. Sweet Jesus, Sal. Look at her. Mutt... hey, Mutt."

"Sugar..."

"*Sugar*? You might as well call me Elvis."

"If you had the soul of an Elvis I would call you Elvis."

"Smells like a chum bucket."

"Maybe that's just the smell that God gave her. Exuberant. That would be the word for it."

Absolutely. A veritable dynamo of decay. Burbles like a busted keg. Exfoliates out across the landscape like a goddamn holy object, smoke on a rope the preacher swings, up and down the aisle, so as to asphyxiate the each of us equally.

"Stupid dog," I say. I grab the hose, rainbow that water up to within a step or two to where she stands. "Look. Lookie-here. I'm right here. Here look."

The dumb mutt, she can't see where she's going, but still manages to steer up into the spray, to stick out her tongue to touch the wetness, to home in on the sound of the my voice.

Sal steps up with the brush. "Come on, girl."

"That dog's gotta learn how to walk in a straight line," I say.

"Like you're the one to teach her?" says Sal.

As if pushed by an invisible wind, Sugar shoulders her way up flush against the cinderblock. Catches her balance. There. That's better. Props herself up as she chugs along now, scratches her starboard side up and down as she goes, kind of circular motion like a block of sandpaper, like a blind whale back-scratching up against the barnacle-encrusted Queen Mary.

"So I'm the one's gotta baby-sit this damn – "

"Good Lord, no. No no. I love you to pieces but you know as well as I do the League of Nations not about to crown you Ambassador to Doglandia. All you gotta do is run her up to the plant and then pick her up in the morning. Boom-boom: done."

Up the drive, Sugar, she waddles, sack of skin all bulgy and

> **" On the other side of the formaldehyde divide you got Sal, Mahatma Gandhi of the panty-hose set, leaping up with them eyebrow tweezers to splint the wing on a flailing mosquito.**

bristly at the same time, like she been shake 'n baked in a bag of iron filings, like she got a magnet slowly somersaulting its way up into her guts, pressing up under the surface, quivering all that fur up into collapsible little crescents and ellipticals, you know, like a bath towel twisted underfoot. She stumbles right into a tangle of hedge clippings.

"Do I look like a zoo-keeper to you?" I jettison the hose. It slithers down the steps, gurgles off into the weeds.

"Now correct me if I'm wrong," says Sal, "but don't that sound a bit posh coming from somebody sleeping on a mattress in the garage?"

"But who's gonna want to sit in that car after – "

"Last time I looked, that car's a company car, you are a company man, and that dog, that dog is a company dog."

"Company mascot you mean."

"Company mascot."

"But I'm the company mascot."

"I am so sorry. What was I thinking? I beg your most magestical pardon. If you would be so kind as to deputize that valet of yours to go fetch up the company.... Unless a little puppy's too much for you to handle. You know, what with you being, well, you being you and all."

"Puppy. You call that mutt a puppy?"

"Eyes like a – "

"One eye."

"But like a puppy. Got the heart of a puppy."

When I reach down to tug Sugar loose, she jams her face up into my fingers, stipples me with the tip of her nose, slathers me with the flat of her tongue, cold and then hot and then cold again. Some kind of ectoplasm come oozing up out of the depths, that's what slobber is – marinate and baconaisse and saliva alfredo -- over and over as if, by the sheer eagerness of her affection, she will somehow, in the end, render me edible.

"Jackson. Listen. Think about it. It's the least you can do."

"The least?"

"And think about the companionship."

"I prefer my friends don't sit around licking their privates."

"Oh that's rich. Mr. Congeniality. You and all them dozens of friends of yours."

I can feel the thump-thump of that melon head of Sugar's up against my kneecap as she maneuvers round to lick the salt from my ankle.

"A dog would be perfect for you. You got none of the complications you get with people."

"Complications?"

"Involvements."

"Involvements."

"You know what I mean."

"Dogs don't get thirsty if that's what you mean."

"That's not what I said."

"I didn't say that you did." I got what you might call a drinking problem. Hardly seems fair, does it? The one thing I'm really good at. You don't hear people saying Einstein had a physics problem, do you?

"Sal. Why would you shuttle her back and forth like that when you could – "

Sal explains. See, on the one side you got Billy (the brother-in-law), second he gets a hamster with even so much as the sniffles – *boom* -- it's off to the taxidermist. On the other side of the formaldehyde divide you got Sal, Mahatma Gandhi of the panty-hose set, leaping up with them eyebrow tweezers to splint the wing on a flailing mosquito.

Now the only way to save Sugar from Billy is to maneuver Sugar into whatever location that Billy is not, meaning home by day, the factory by night.

"Bad idea," I say.

"Says who?"

"Six thousand pound oven and a spoonful of dog. What could possibly go wrong?"

"No dog, no car," says Sal. "That's the deal."

"But – "

"Here." She hands me a box of Natura-Grain – shot of this Golden Labrador leaping up out of a wheat field and into the blue of the breeze.

"Cereal?"

"Organics."

"What? Vegi-ham? Rice Crispies? What?"

"Organs. It's the organs got all the protein – like liver. Ever heard of liver? That's why they call it organics."

"Who the hell is they?"

"Doctor's orders." She gives the box a shake. Sounds like a gravel soufflé. Doctor's not a doctor, not a vet, not even a taxidermist, no. Neighbor's got a buddy knows a guy breeds birddogs, swears by it, shreds all this crap up into their regular food.

Gotta be a word to capture the flavor of this whole enterprise – and by that I mean not Sugar alone, but every last one of us here strapped onto this whirligig of a planet. Rusted? Busted? Not broken irreparably – that would be too easy, no, but *stuck*. Stuck with a promise of perfection that's always and forever just short of the means to fulfill it -- the bow without the string, the crippled wing, the rowboat stuck out there in the middle of the meadow. It's like we all been permanently epoxied into a shape that bears no resemblance to the dashing photo on the front of the box, to the set of instructions – Japanese, English, Hottentot, Urdu – slid up under the lid with (like a Gideon's Bible at a stripper's retreat) such a touching naiveté. A kludge, that's what we are, every damn one of us.

Sal slips a muzzle down onto Sugar's snout and fusses with the straps. "There you go, Baby. Mama's got a treat for you." Up under the muzzle she maneuvers this little bullet of something sorta green, you know -- pond scum or alginate, some kind of rabbit aperitif, but Sugar, she's too busy chewing on the leather strap. Got all the personality of a pot roast, that dog, but dammed if she don't possess like what they say in them commercials for Le Cordon Bleau – an exquisite sense of taste.

* * *

I lean over the car with the bait in hand. Behind me the red neon *Sleepy Shack* sign clicks on, fizzes up against the gray sky, starts to hum. I shake off the wrapper, strip the Whopper down to a shingle of beef, dangle it out over the floorboards. Sugar she's sniffing – I'm up over her blind side and she knows, she can tell there's something tasty out there, but spatula-ed into the back seat like that, all folded up onto herself like an omelet, she can't seem to manage much more than bobble-de-bobble, forward and back, forward and back, like a rocking horse with nothing but the belly left to gallop on.

"Okay dog. Here. Here girl. Stupid. Stupid. Here, stupid, here. No I know – you don't speak English. Of course not, no, that'd be too easy."

Okay. So I gotta crawl back in to fetch her. Carpe Deum. By the time I get her squeegied up over the steering wheel I'm about ready to melt. Not from that blubbery embrace – the skin to skin, the beat of her heart against the beat of my own -- no, but from the smell. Distilled essence of dogginess.

"No, no. Bad girl. Get that tongue... no. No, no – stop it, stop, stop. Stop breathing..."

You always hear about the smell of the great outdoors, but the thing about the great outdoors is that it's spread out all over the great outdoors – salt air through a stand of pines, cut grass and burnt ember, potpourri of cat-tails and topsoil and leaf mold in the morning mist. You cram all them spices down into one square foot, it's like taking a bite out of a bouillon cube -- and that's just your over-the-counter doggy broth. Haven't even stirred in yet that particular stew of ingredients labeled *Cachet de Sugar*. Fish oil and slime mold and Pterodactyl breath.

Trilobite dung and Mastodon cud and pulverized essence of crocodile glands, all sautéed up into a tasty little fur-covered croquet.

I squeeze up out the door, samba-style, Sugar in my arms. Strange how lonely I been that even this qualifies as an embrace, cozy kind of violence, like boxers in a clench at the bell, all rubbery and huggable and sweet. Sugar slides down over my rib-cage, blooms out into a split, butters her way down the whole length of my leg.

"Get up," I hiss. "Get up, stupid..." I brush the hamburger up over her snout and then frisbee it off into the woods. "Go girl. Go!"

She licks my shoelaces. Only part of her that moves is the tongue. "Sugar!" I give her a little nudge in the butt.

There now. That's it. Sugar, she don't start that tail of hers by wagging it. Damn starter is broken, so first thing you see is kind of a, more of a tremor than a wag.

"Go, Sugar, go! Go girl!"

Little quiver in the hips set off by... God knows. Maybe there's some invisible transference of energy going on, some cocktail waitress in Topeka orgasms and the seismic vibrations buzz down the Winnebago springs to lodge in the gas pipes beneath the truck stop parking lot till that last gasp and shimmy sends them shooting through the aquifer, down I-Four, South Orange Blossom Trail exit 42, up and down the undulating Booties Drive-In turf, a-rattling under the chain link, and out past the Suntek loading dock and onward through the woods, buzzing the bark, crackling up under the carpet of pine needles and running right up onto the backlot of *Sleepy Shack* and into the tender loins of Sugar, the Wonder Dog.

"That's it, girl! You got it!"

There's that little kick to get her started, stick of licorice tick-tick-tick of the tail, pendulum that sets the whole machine into motion.

* * *

Back at the room I got just enough time to hit the shower and baptize myself with the condiments of love -- Lavoris and Arid and Hai-Karate in the commando aerosol pack.

Damn that dog. *How the hell should I know, Sal?* is what I'll say, *Scout's honor. Damn dog just up and ran away.* Thrill-seeker – that's what she is. Shoots out there into the wild -- the slurp and the lick and the poke-poke-poke of the road kill, all that doggy crap. Doggie crap, people crap – it's all the same. Sal's got her movie mags and her -- whatever you call that chamomile sauce she butters herself with. Me? I got a bottle, sure, but I also got a woman. Interlocking puzzle piece of a woman. All of that soft geometry on it's way to meet me, bumper me, belly me up into a brand new universe where the wind sings, the water dances, the mosquito greets the newborn with a sugary kiss.

You can just feel it, can't you? The whole world -- like it's just vibrating underfoot? And after all, ain't that what got us all here in the first place? People orgasming (is that the word?) all over the place, over the city, overseas, Jews and Arabs, Mennonite Babes in hand-knit bonnets and Argentinean dictators with their epaulettes quivering. Four billion people in the world and we got what, how many hundreds of millions strapped onto that roller coaster right now, right this very second, zooming up to achieve escape velocity -- that flash in the brain, that tsunami in the cerebral cortex – see? Simple like a dog is simple, right? Right? That's why marriage is such a crock. Gotta be tethered to something, sure, but the trick is to play the comet, blaze in there every now and again, sure, spin round the sun, sure, but never so close you lose your momentum. Gotta remember, see, a comet's a ball of ice. What looks like a blaze – an obliteration's what that is.

The appointed hour passes. When I hear the knocking – light, as if the door were made of paper – I stash the bottle, whisper out over the carpet barefoot. That's the way to woo a woman. You gotta glide up into range, you know, like on the radio in the dark when you turn the dial, sift your way up through the static to find the perfect tune. *My girl, talking 'bout my girl, ba-doopa-doopa* – I crack the door open, greet the moon, tip out over the threshold to drink in the night.

*Raspitt-raspitt-raspitt.*

Jesus H. Hubert Humphrey Christ.

\* \* \*

Sal's got a smoke in one hand, stubble of half-smokes in the pie-tin on her desk, bubble of smoke up under the ceiling tiles like a soufflé.

I step into the office, fingers all fuzzed up as I rub and I rub, try to unspackle the fur from off of the belly of my shirt. Hail all hail the Wonder Dog. Got her nested down into that old tractor tire out front, that ginormous rubber turd of a decorative planter Sal never got around to actually plantifying. Trust me, my friends, and hearken unto my word: damn sight easier to bed down a woman than to bed down a dog.

Sal, she's trying to wedge one of those pogo-stick curtain rods up into the cinderblock frame of the window, but it keeps popping loose.

"It's a goddamn factory, Sal. Not *The Little House On The Prairie.*"

She turns. The rod springs out of her hand, disappears into the clutter. "Oh. Some girl on the line for you. She won't say her name."

"Not to you she won't."

"If it's who I think it is..."

"Go kiss the damn dog, Sal."

Sal lingers as I make my way to the phone. Tilts into the doorframe with her purple clipboard up into that 10-2 position favored by safe drivers everywhere, pretending to read as she spot-checks the polish on her Lee Press-On Nails and reconnoiters down to the pedicure protruding from the bow of them Gucci pumps. Exchequer to the Throne, Duchess of the Provinces of Aquitaine and Double-Insulated Therma-formered Lexan Single-Unit Flange Couplings, officiating in absentia over even the dust motes in their little *pas de deux* through the empty air. "Don't be tying up the lines now with personal calls," she says. "That's the company phone."

I pick up the receiver, give Sal the heave-ho.

I can tell by the silence it's Angie.

"I'm sorry," she says at last.

"Don't tell me why you didn't come," I say. "I know why you didn't come. You're thinking he needs you more than I do, right?"

"You realize how *fff*-ed up that sounds?" she says.

*Fff*-ed. That's the way she says it. *But that takes all the uck out of it* I'd say, I'd always tell her. *That's the best part, the uck.* "I know how it sounds," I say, "but am I right?"

"If it's a contest as to who is the most pathetic..."

"Then I'd win," I say. "I'm the winner."

Now she's laughing. "You are so pathetic."

"No. No, I am the most pathetic. Top dog. I guarantee, I promise, I swear that I am more *fff*ed-up than he will ever be."

Now, the whole point of a jest is not to dislodge the truth from its sacred perch, but like a pole-vaulter who clears the bar, to brush it with the hem of the sleeve, ping it with a shoelace, pluck it so it quivers. That's what you do with the truth. Zip-zop off a molecule or two as you snowflake over to land in the pit. The last thing you want is to smack up onto it, crotch-first.

She starts to cry. Jesus Christ. Cry?

"I can't keep doing this," she says.

"Then leave him," I say.

"If I had something to go to..."

"You telling me that I'm not something?"

"You could be something."

"Could be. But right now, no, right? Right now not enough of a something?"

"That's not what I mean."

"Okay then. What do you mean?"

I tug on the curly black cord bobbing up out of the avalanche of beauty mags that cover the desk. Seeker-outer of the mysteries of the cosmos, that'd be Sal. Cosmotologist at heart.

"I mean," she says, "just where *are* you? Where're you at right now, anyway?"

"At?"

"You gotta have a direction. I need some kind of direction."

What am I, Magellan? It's all I can do to just navigate myself into the upright and locked position. I tug the cord – careful, so as not to jar this pile of booty Sal's been scraping together. Mags all broken open to the rigid inserts where the secret itch resides, the scent – *Tabu* and *Chanel* and *Seduction* – scratched up off of the page by the scarlet tip of her nail, stirred up over the incinerated air of a dozen ashtrays -- the mug and the vase and the empty bandaid tin, the screw-top lid to the peanut butter and the clam-shell lid to the diaphram (all melty and uterish and pink), even the foil from a Hershey bar molded now, squashed down to a bowl no deeper than the dent of a thumb.

"My heart's in the right place," I say.

"Your heart is a hand grenade."

Then everything happens at once. Sal's voice from down the hall (*Sugar! Sugar!*), out the front door shouting (*Sugar! Sugar!*), then back in again. *Sugar! Sugar!*

"You don't have a clue," says Angie, "do you?"

"I gotta go," I say.

"Where the hell that heart of yours – "

"Gotta go, I gotta go..."

"Don't you hang up on me."

"But it's not a hang up if I tell you I'm hanging up. I'm hanging up. I gotta hang up."

"I – "

I hang up.

The whole plant echoes with the sound of Sal. Cursing. Calling out in that dipsy-doodle voice, you know – you conjure children with? Clatter of boxes. Clack of the heels. Sugar's gone missing. From somewhere back of the therma-former, paint-booth, breaker box, I hear Sal, the Voice of God, calling down the heavens: "You! This is all your fault!"

Me, that's who the *you* is. I break for the door of the loading dock, open just enough of a sliver to where I can stop, drop, and roll up under the steel guillotine, onto the ramp, and into the glare of the headlights of Billy's car. Now when you're stuck between the anvil and the hammer, the last thing you want to do is advertise your position, so you squat, see, like you're just now easing into a smoke break, you know, like normal. The normal routine being Billy plus Don the partner (D&B I call them) come tooling up the drive in Billy's dead grandma's Chevy Impala (the whole inheritance by the way, the only part she couldn't drink) having just hooked a potential client, potential the operative word, potential being, in Billy's Bible, the *single most important ingredient for success.* Yes sir, Billy. Potential, like the single most important ingredient for an inflatable life raft is air. Thank God we're blessed with air. Warehouse overflowing with air. Air stacked up on top of air, right up to the ceiling. *Say Billy* I'd say, *say didn't you just post a guard dog out here to keep an eye on all that air? Big mistake* I'd say, *Big --*

But not now, no, now that we all been sugarized. Now the very second D&B come busting up the ramp, buzzing with possibilities – spit and polish suits and Sunday cowboy boots, showered and shaved and stinking of Listerine and Old Spice, Square-dance tie tacks and brand-new attaché cases (two for one at Kmart) -- who meets them at the door but Sal, keeper of lost causes and Jesus Christ Junior to any random lump of fur. Sal, who demands they turn around and go back out and find Sugar. Sugar's gone. Wandered off or somebody stole her.

"Stole her?" says Billy as we march out into the parking lot.

"Stole the guard dog?" says Don. "How do you steal a guard dog?

Billy plants his feet, stares out at the dark horizon. "That thing got a, what? Got a leash, or what?"

"Look what I found," says Sal, stepping up behind me. *Thwack.* I spin away, my left ear blazing, like I been clipped by a flame-thrower. "Look familiar?" She shakes it under my nose like it was me should be the one to wear it, then clamors up onto the big tire to reconnoiter the territory. Snap goes the heel of the shoe. She pitches backwards into Billy's arms, but he's so big it's like nothing, like she was a doll you gotta just stand her back up again.

"Too dark to see a damn thing," says Don. "You gotta follow

your nose."

It don't take but a breath. The smell of fried chicken comes rolling in through the chain link fence that borders the drive-in, the far screen of which we can just glimpse from here.

Sal runs – hobbles really -- back to fetch a pair of flats. *Tip-toe, click, Tip-toe, click.* Shish-ka-bobbed up onto the stiletto of the good heel, flap-flapping along for the ride, is a magazine ad, one of them inserts. *Everygreen's* what it says, glint of green like a bed of clover. *Evergreen. Evergreen.* Whatever Evergreen's peddling – the clean, the pristine, that notion of Sal's to remodel the cosmos into a slab of perfume you slide through the leaves of a *Vogue* or a *Glamour* – the exact opposite of all that'd have to be *Bootie's.*

*Boom-chicka, boom-chicka, boom-chicka,* Sheba-Baby, Blackula, Shaft and Mandingo. *Bootie's Drive-In.* Superfly and Cleopatra Jones. Two bucks a car but not everybody's got a car, so the neighbors toss their lawn-chairs over the fence and squeeze in through the broken links to reassemble amoeba-like in the gaps between the cars. The maximum comfort crowd spill out into our parking lot, the crème de la crème who gather round the dumpster we share with Red's Auto Body. Jam a broke sofa up against the chain link, tuck a bucket of chicken under your arm, kick back to enjoy the show. Tetanus shot and a good rope, you can rappel up to the luxury box on the dumpster roof, theater of the stars, study spectrographic emissions from Alpha Centari as filtered through an empty bottle of Boone's Farm Strawberry Wine. Boone's Farm Strawberry Wine, now that's a wine in a hurry, wine on the cutting edge. You don't age a Boone's Farm wine. Hell, it takes nine minutes for light from the sun to reach the earth, who the hell's got the time for that, and for what? A grape?

"Spread out," says Billy.

"Don't make a scene," says Don as we approach the fence. Billy stops to fetch a beach towel out the back seat of his car and then, stiff as a store mannequin, Sal and Don behind him, unbuttons his cardboardy suit coat to wriggle through the break in the fence.

"I got your back," says me, thinking, even as I say it, *that's what they say in the movies.*

Sal heads out along the perimeter, where the drunks and the rag-pickers gather. The three of us fan out among the rows, start working our way toward the screen. Already I'm calibrating just how fast I can run with these boots on. Take "white" and "square" and fold them up together, that's what you get in D&B, whiteness cubed, brittle as a biscuit, couple of clacketty sugar cubes swallowed up into that pot of hot black Bootie's Drive-In Movie Theater brew.

How many billion places to hide out here? *Sugar... Sugar....* Off in the distance the pines they brush up against the stars, swing out in a solid wall round the curve of the fence-line, seems like a mile away but it's a trick of the moon is what it is, simplifies it all down to a silhouette that screens out the rest of the world -- the fractured skull of the silo out back of the Rinker Plant, the busted steeple of the Blessed Cathedral of Truth, the corrugated tin roof of the abandoned lumberyard.

There she is – Sal. I can just catch the glint of a flashlight bobbing up over the ridges, down, up, further and further away. A valley of shadows is what it is, open at one end to Sun-Tek and to Red's, where the junkers rust and the tires pillar up over the fence, open at the other to the gravel track that zig-zags out through the pines and then behind the screen to the marquee that fronts the road, (... *ooties*) with the missing *B*, the plexi-red letters *Cleo Jones + 2* clapped up onto the lightbox like a ransom note, the tollbooth where – I can just picture it now -- the pimply kid sleeps with his cheeks puttied up onto the cash box, and the fat-as-a-roll-of-film tickets spiral out, like the peel of an apple, down the slope of his Levi's.

*Sugar... Sugar...* I stop to breathe. Off in the distance, tucked up under the projection booth at the heart of it all is this little island of light, cinderblock bunker where they shave the ice and peddle the treats and the steam of the oven powders out the slats in back to paint the air white. A doggy heaven of popcorn blossoms and griddle grease, cinnamon and pepper and the burnt cheese at the rim of the pizza. I follow the trail, follow my nose till the earth turns just enough to jostle the air again, to send it reaping out across the furrows now left, then right, to scatter the smells of all the contraband in all the cars -- the reefer, the beer, the sausage and the cornbread crimped in the foil and then crackled open, broken, and then again the wind again, crossways now, the glaze of the Krispy Kreme stuck to the sleeve, the jalapeño tacquito snapped at the spine, the short ribs and the peach pits and the chicken all swaddled in butcher-block. And then back again, like it was the earth itself breathing in and breathing out. The smell of shit, of earthworms and mushrooms, pine sap and turtle turds, cat piss and burnt rubber, and even something maybe just barely tangible there, couple three molecules of road-kill (vintage stuff, turn of the century), steamed up out of the cracked asphalt a mile away. Damn dog could be anywhere.

Sal's out beyond the snack bar, flit-flit-flit of red between the cars. Don's up ahead, a half-dozen cars away. Stops at the foot of the sign. *Row Six.* Billy steps into the pool of light. Got the beach towel looped over his shoulders, scrolled up into kind of a cable, kind of a makeshift leash. He says something to Don. Don nods his head, launches back out into the darkness. Billy motions me over. Not a boss thing – this more like a family affair – but I obey. Billy, he grew up on a farm, see, all them creatures coming and going, gives him a kind of authority here.

"This is between us, right?" he says.

I nod my head. Whatever the *this* is, it's a man thing, and I'm a man, right?

He peels back the towel at one end to reveal a rope as thick as my wrist. "She won't feel a thing," he says. Wraps the towel back around the rope, gives it a gentle squeeze. "Won't leave a mark."

I nod to show I understand, keep nodding, nodding, the way men do when they come to an understanding, like it's something apart from me, this nod, public signal of a secret intent, buoy in a bay bobbing with the tide. Billy disappears back into the rows.

It's not a betrayal, is it? How can it be a betrayal when there's nothing that – she's a creature like any other creature, right? Not but a blip in the billion upon billion of blips that ever lived, that ever peppered the crust of the earth, that ever bubbled around and around the rotisserie sun.

I strike out in the opposite direction, headlong in pursuit of a place where not a dog would ever dare to stray, some kind of Sugar-free zone.

"Sugar..." I mouth it without breathing, as if to breath would be to conjure her up. Maybe they won't find her. Maybe no one'll find her. Maybe Gina Lollobrigida will float up out the back seat of a convertible with her arms reaching out to reel me into the bosomy softness of her soul. That's what the dark is for, right? To dream? And after all, that's what, that's where – from out of the darkness – we all of us, we came from, right?

I sweep around the back row, curb the light up off the windows where the couples curl just out of sight, pretzel down into the upholsterish folds of a Coupe Deville or a Buick Centura, bail out over the bucket seats and into the cavernous hold of a Grande Torino hatchback to buckle in the heat, couple in the dark, bake in the moonlight up under the slick-as-a-casket dome of the glass. *Pussy-mobile*, that's what Billy calls it: the soft on the inside of these cars, the leather like butter that yields to the shape of the body, the seat that unbends to a bed, the white piping that traces the curves and the valleys like a trail for the finger to follow, like lace on a pastry. The *fertile crescent* is what Dad used to call this place, all of them girls, year after year, knocked up in all of them portable boudoirs, baby no bigger than the head of a pin just waiting to burst into bloom: the soon-to-be senators and astronauts and Miss Vidalia Onion Queens pop-gunned into existence halfway through a triple-feature bull-dozed out the back forty of somebody's orange grove.

I'm down on one knee, kind of a half-squat, half-shuffle as I paint the flanks of the cars with my little circle of light, the tricked-out buggies with the white-walls and the woven spokes, the wind-scoops and the fins and the hood-pieces all chromified up into trophies. Rams-head. Swordfish. The hammer of Thor and the beak of the hawk and the snap of the tiny bronze banner, stiff as a triscuit, like the flag on the face of the moon.

I listen for a sound in the distance, out over the creak of the cars, the wind in the trees, the bluesy music buzzing out of every window. Sal maybe. Or Billy, that whistle of his. Is there such a thing as a good death? Look at all of these cars here half again as old as I am, and all crusted with... what do you call it? Them little black ampersands? Love-bugs. That's it. Sucked up into the backwash of a passing semi, tangoed out over the steamy blacktop, squashed in the moment of bliss.

A voice at my ear, kinda low to the ground, like a road-grater.
"You looking for somebody?"

I start, drop the flashlight, look up at the back door of the
Caddie, the open window, the black of a rectangle rimmed with silver.
"I – "

"Don't touch the car."

I pull my hand away, frog-walk back a step.

"You little shit. You looking at my car?"

"No, I'm just -- "

"You looking at my girl?"

"Just looking for my dog is all. I gotta look -- "

"Look like you taking a shit. You taking a shit?"

"I can't..."

"You can't what? Can't take a shit? Can't get the shit out?"
The door-lock pops up. "Maybe I could beat the shit out of you? How
would that be?"

Somehow I'm back onto my feet, don't even know how it
happens, but I'm walking, clunky like a puppet, tripping out over the
stubble. Crunch of gravel behind me. I break into a run. Dumb like a
dog I run. Running – that's a kind of falling, right? Through the dark,
yes, and even when, behind me, the foot-falls drop away, I run, simple
like a dog is simple, to the center, to the island of light. Back of the
snack-bar – I can just make it out – there's a patch of tall grass that
rises up into the empty just under the beam of the projector.

"Sugar!" I call out in earnest now. "Sugar!" I close in on the
beacon till it comes to a point, a... not a cone, no, too tame, but a – what
do you call it? Vortex. More like the mouth of a twister than a hunk
of geometry, what with the swirl of the colors and the shadows in a
scramble and the rhythmical din of the sprocketry. Take the tick of a

clock and kick it up into a spin, that's the sound of a reel of film trilling out into the hot air, kid with a card in the spokes of his bike, Jack of diamonds clipped onto the tines, pick of a banjo *ticka-ticka-ticka-ticka.*

I look out along the beam to that single spot the cars they all take   aim at, the screen that booms up into the black like a slice of a slab of the moon itself, crackling with light. Sal's closing in on the snack bar from the one side, D&B from the other, they all them converging. Fifty-foot high Cleopatra Jones flashes up against the sky, her coffee-colored cleavage big as a Macy's Day parade float broken loose and bounding down the white suburban streets, crushing all resistance beneath her enormously delicious embrace. *Sugar... Sugar... Here, Sugar... Come here, girl...*

Then I hear something. Back behind this big old four-door Buick, color of a dirty piano key, cookies-and-cream colored rolling raft of a love-mobile rocking from stem to stern, shaken by the earth into wakefulness, stirred within by the chafe-chafe-chafing of skin upon skin. You don't dream about a car, no. A car's the thing you climb into to dream about everything else.

*Raspitt... raspitt... raspitt...*

"Sugar... Sugar?"

Everybody dies, right? You get just so many snapshots before the reel runs dry, the spool it flutters – the son of a bitch – flutters out empty. The question: which one these, out of that whole damn avalanche of billions upon billions, do I decide to keep? You do whatever the hell you want, but for me, I take a snapshot and hold it right here, right at the top of the coaster where the guardrails drop and the gravity evaporates and everybody onboard keen to get some one thing they can only get right here, right this second: Sal keen to get Sugar, D&B keen to get the hell out of there, Cleopatra Jones keen to shoot the double-dealing Honkie-Ass D.A., the Bootie cliental keen to cheer Cleopatra shoot the double-dealing Honkie-Ass D.A., the Boone's Farm contingent keen to shoot slow-motion star-ward on a geyser of strawberry wine, and not but a shout away, Sal, as she threshes out through the crowd at the snack bar, Billy not but a handful of cars between us as he doubles back on the lookout for me, me, keen in the dark here to signal the choice I make here, where she is right now, Sugar the Wonder Dog, keeled up on her back, legs kicking in the air, quivering from nose to tail like a new-born pup dropped head-first into a bowl of warm milk, keen to be swallowed up in that delicious Drive-In dirt, a dog no more but more than a dog, buried in a bliss of chicken bones and slickery ribs and tick-tick-ticking tail counting out a music only she can hear. Damn that dog. Damn that dog. I don't know what it means, what the hell it's supposed to mean, that picture, half the people in it dead and gone now, Billy gone, Sugar gone, outside that circle of light me standing in the darkness but still looking, looking on, taking it all in, but that picture, I close my eyes – don't ask me again because I'll never tell you – but why is it that that picture is the picture I picture when I picture love?

*Sugar* was featured originally in a Live Audience/Radio/Podcast/ Chapbook Publication in partnership with Big Fiction, Bremelo Press, and the Seattle Office of Arts & Culture (August 2015).

# HELLO DARKNESS, I'M DAD

## BY CLAY WATERS

### *So how do you guys like my cowboy hat?*

In the old days they called this a 10-gallon hat. A gallon is a, ah skip it, there'll be no learning today, boys and girls, ladies and germs. Let me just tilt it to the left a tad. There we go. Debbie, that old wife of mine, would have called this a "jaunty angle." Hope you had a good breakfast. I gave you double scoops of oatmeal. Hope it filled your gullet, pardner. Today is a big day, yessir. Yes Jason, I'm aware it's not a very good cowboy accent. Hey wait, how would you know!

We're going to have lots of fun today, yessir. First we're going to color a picture of a tiger. And then we have a real treat for you buckaroos: Ice cream and Coca-Cola! There we go, there's a little life out there.

I've got another surprise for you. Doc will be rising out of the basement to join us. Hey, don't everyone clap at once! I've got a bunch of crayons too, 27 different colors, though some are kind of nubby. Go ahead Aaron, start passing them around.

Shoot-fire, I almost forgot about the puppets, I mean, Dr. Dog and Miss Meow! Where is my head today? We'll talk to them soon too. Now Jenny, that gal was good with the puppets: Remember Teddy, the Armadillo from Amarillo? Old Teddy was a hoot and a half, wasn't he? I'm not as good as Jenny but I'll give it my best. I used to think this kind of thing was silly when the other grownups did it. Now I see the point.

Let's hope this little light comes on. It's going to be a long hour if the projector doesn't work. I'm using generator power, which usually makes Doc mad, but today he's giving me a pass. Ah, there we go. I've got 18 slides set up, one for each one of you guys, plus a special one for the very last. But you have to do what I say when we get to that one, OK?

Yep, you're right, Amelia, I forgot I was a cowboy again. I never was good at this sort of thing. Maybe the worst. But everyone else has left the building. Taking care of kids after something like this is not for everyone. Not for anyone. Maybe you don't know how bad I am at this, but some of you older ones like Timmy know it could be done better.

Ok, who wants to hear some jokes? "What do you call a bear with no teeth? A gummy bear." I'd taken that one out of the rotation because some of you guys' teeth were falling out.

"What kind of jewelry do rabbits wear?14-carat gold." I know food jokes make you hungrier, but carrots aren't much of a food.

I am telling a lot of jokes today, Amber-Lynn. When in doubt, pile up the distractions. That's what Jenny told me before she left.

No Mike, I don't think Jenny's coming back.

Hey, look up here at the screen! There's Mr. Crayon and Mr. Seal! They wouldn't want you to be sad, would they? There's always a reason to be happy. Just keep looking hard, to the very end. You know what my reason is? You guys! Did you know that?

Yes it is chilly in here, Temetria, sorry about that. What's that Millie? You found Jenny's purple dress stuffed in the broken windowpane? Maybe she left it there so you wouldn't get cold. Yes, she might be cold now. But that's the kind of person Jenny w--is. Always thinking of others. That's why I married her here, well, kind of. I married Debbie first, before the cookie caved. Long story. Sure I miss her, Jeff. I miss them both. But...No Millie, I don't know why the other grownups all left.

You say you know why, Timmy? Maybe keep it to yourself, ok there, pardner?

Should we go outside to look for Jenny? No, sorry, Alison, I don't have the strength to corral you all. And I want you all here to watch the Alpaca Clips. We named them after something you said, did you know that, Alison? Apocalypse, Alpaca Clips? It's what we grownups call an inside joke. That means it's not funny.

Whoa, pardners! I almost didn't say good morning! Good Morning, Ladies and Germs. Do you guys remember Ryder didn't like hearing about germs because Lucy left after she got that cut and that's why we stopped passing around scissors?

Well my big hand is on the 10 already so we better keep rolling. We've got to watch our time today.

Yes, I guess I am speaking kind of weird this morning, Toby. I guess I'm listening for Doc's feet on the stairs. Things in the basement are moving a little bit faster than we planned so he's going to join us for a little party with ice cream and Coca-Cola. How does that sound? The light's bright up here with the projector so I can't see your beautiful faces this morning. Cool slides, huh? It's just like watching TV.

No Jason, I know it really isn't. Geez, you're hard to please, aren't you?

Alright, let's try the next slide. Let's see, we've got a boy, a girl, and a dog doing a crossword puzzle that spells the names of the kids' meals at Ruby Tuesdays. And there's also a smiling owl saying "Hoo says food can't be fun?" The joke is that an owl goes "Hoo!" and...never mind.

I scavenged restaurants for these things in the early days. Wasting precious gasoline, as one jackass grownup reminded me. Anything with a smile on it I salvaged. Kids menus, birthday bags, lottery tickets. Some from here too, it's really not a bad library for a little Baptist school. Don't worry, I'm not going to read a story today. Today is all about having fun.

Why did we even bother with reading? I'm no teacher. And when I got here I was about three seconds ahead of a cave man about practical stuff. And look at me now! Siphoning gasoline and everything.

Yes, my beard does itch, Temetria. I haven't had a hot bath in about 28 months so I kind of itch all over. I would have cut it off but you know what we say about playing with scissors, right? Too risky. I guess I was just trying to look like Doc. I could shave it off now, but I'd rather spend the time here with you guys.

Do you need a cough drop, Ryan? Sorry, *Ryder*. Ryan was my boy. My lucky boy. He didn't have to live through this. Ok, Let's see what's on the next slide. A happy cat with a happy fish. Hmm. Can they both be happy, I wonder?

Oh geez, what have I done? Yes Susie, I know Happy the cat ran away. Sorry. Please don't cry. Yes, we do lose a lot of pets, that's a solid observation, Jason. No, I don't know how they get out. The same way the grownups got out, maybe? But let's not talk about all that right now.

What's Happy doing now, Susie? Well, I bet he's having fun chasing squirrels. Ever notice all colleges are really proud of their particular squirrels? No, I imagine you haven't.

Hey here's a joke, *"What's brown and sticky? A stick."*

Oh you've heard that one, have you Millie? I bet you have. Don't you guys want to finish coloring your tigers? Guess not. Well, we'll just whip through these last slides, no more dawdling, right?

Go outside? Sorry Oliver, but it's important we stay inside today. I know it's sad down here with no windows but you're not missing much, trust me. Everything feels cold and dark, even when it's sunny. You have to figure there are other survivors somewhere, but...man it's quiet.

I dream about you guys, you know. Every night it's the same. We're all together, everyone who has ever been in this room, all 53 of you. I don't even have to count, I just know. Except we're not down in this dump but in the longest, tallest plane ever. Kind of like a flying hotel. A hotel is a building with -- ah skip it.

What's that Oliver? You're right, that is something new up here. Glad you noticed. That's a portrait of me and Debbie and my boy Ryan. I tucked it under my arm and carried it all the way here, oh 28 months ago. That same jackass said I couldn't keep it because anything a sick person touched could still harbor the virus that caused the Cave-in but I ignored him. Caveolae cells, who knew they'd turn out to be so important? That's where we got the word "Cave-in" from, in case you guys didn't figure it out.

I remember trying to cheer myself up when the thing first hit and we were all locked in our homes but the internet still worked -- you remember the internet, right? What did you watch your cartoons on? Anyway there were these clips with this perky girl, a grownup woman really, with a curly red wig. And she was always smiling and she had dog puppets and cat puppets and bird puppets.

Well in her very last clip she gathered all her puppets around her because they were afraid and told them that things might seem scary but they shouldn't be scared, that things would turn out OK. She was still smiling too, all the way. Turns out we were right to be scared. But you know what? She said the right thing.

She'd be good at this.

Sometimes I wonder what happened to her. Maybe she was a freak like us with rogue genes.

Did you know I had the idea of raising a troupe of little scientists out of you guys, to help Doc find a cure? I know he smells funny Jake, yes. That's formaldehyde. But he cares about you just like I do, you know, that's how he shows it, by staying down there working hard. We're like your Dads, kind of. Your two apocalypse Dads.

Well yeah, we're not like your read Dads, or even like Paul was, that's right, Twyla. No one could be like Paul. He loved you guys and you loved him back. Remember Paul saying, "Same bat time, same bat channel"? Now that was a fun show.

> **❝ I know he smells funny Jake, yes. That's formaldehyde. But he cares about you just like I do, you know, that's how he shows it, by staying down there working hard.**

I bet some of you older kids have those kinds of memories, like going to Disney and getting pizza or going to the beach. I wonder if remembering the good times makes it all better or worse.

I didn't have any help from any of the gals and we're out of everything and the vegan cookbook in the library wasn't any help. So think of it more like ice cream flavored soup. I'm not sure any kid here has tasted ice cream for real, actually. That takes the pressure off.

Let's just take a little pause here before the last slide.

The door's locked Thomas, sorry. I'm not going to have time to chase down 18 children. Just hold it for another few minutes, OK?

"What do you call cheese that isn't yours? Nacho cheese! What did the janitor say when he jumped out of the closet? Supplies! Why don't cannibals eat clowns? Because they taste funny."

Doesn't anyone want to finish their tiger?

OK, I can sense tears in the offing so I guess that's enough from me. Maybe Dr. Dog and Miss Meow have something they'd like to say? Let's see if they do!

Wait a second, let me get these things straight over my hands. Bet Jenny stayed up all night thinking up those names, huh? Looks like Miss

Meow has seen better days, but haven't we all.

Hello Dr. Dog and Miss Meow! How are you this morning? Stupid question isn't it? Well, fellas, my friends out there in the dark have some things on their mind and I wondered, Miss Meow, if you might be able to help them, being a cat and all. Miss Meow, do you know where Happy the cat is, right now?

What's that you say? That Happy is over the Rainbow Bridge? You say Happy's up with Oscar and Moxie and all the others that ran away? Really now? Well that sounds alright, doesn't it, guys?

And what does Dr. Dog say?

Well, he says that everyone else is over there too, your parents and brothers and sisters and friends, and they don't want you to be sad for them, because we're going to see them all real soon.

Anything else you wanted to say, Miss Meow?

Just that Daddy Dave tried his best.

Gee, thanks Miss Meow. I'm gratified to hear that.

Ok, let me get these things off. Don't cry, guys, it's OK. Sorry about the voices. I know I didn't sound like a cat, or a dog, or a cowboy. I let my emotions get to me. I hope I said some good things, like the girl in the wig.

You guys were awfully quiet today. It's like you know something's up. That's the most annoying thing to ask a kid, isn't it? "Why are you so quiet?" And then you have to start jabbering just to keep Dad happy. Anyway, soon we'll have some ice cream and wash it down with Coca-Cola. If we're lucky it'll still have some fizz left.

I'm really hoping for ice cream huh? Try not to be disappointed. Doc's taking longer than I'd have thought but he'll bring it up soon and then I'll get the Coke and then -- don't cry Bria, it's almost over. I've yeed my last hah.

Whoa! Speak of the devil. Knock knock, must be the Doc. None other than our old friend Dr. Sean Sanders, U.S. Army, came up to join us with the ice cream no doubt.

Now you guys do me a favor, alright? Just concentrate on this sweet little baby alpaca on the screen while I let Doc in and get the Coca-Cola.

Alpacas are sweet little things, aren't they? Maybe they still are somewhere, who knows?

Guys, before we do this, I just wanted to let you all know that.... that...wait, where's the ice cream? What am I looking at, Doc? What's in the cage? Is that the cat? Is that Happy? Living and breathing!? He got better? Does that mean...the last one worked? Maybe? Perhaps? Hey look guys, Doc found Happy! Nice to see you smile, Doc. Sure, put him down. Be gentle with him, kids, Happy's looking a little peaked. So is the Doc. Brian, go get Happy some scraps of oatmeal and some water, I bet he's starving. And maybe a bath, he smells like Doc too.

Ignore the trash bags and rope, kiddos, that was for something that didn't come to pass. Doc must have spilled the ice cream on the way, so maybe we'll have it some other time. Fair warning guys, your meals might be on the skimpy side tomorrow. We kind of went all out today. I'll have to scavenge outside, maybe with a little help, huh, Tim?

See you tomorrow, kids! Same bat time, same bat channel!

9 781955 783132